WELCOME TO AMERICA

ReadersMagnet, LLC
10620 Treena Street, Suite 230 | San Diego, California, 92131 USA
1.619. 354. 2643 | www.readersmagnet.com

WELCOME TO AMERICA

LUIS ZAENSI

CONTENTS

CHAPTER ONE

GREGORIO MEETS TONY

New Jersey, March 1970. Gregorio Romano opens his business of repairing small and medium boats on the banks of the Maurice River. His daughter Lucia is a young woman with frizzy blond hair. She works as the General Manager. She takes care of the accounting, payroll, shipping and receiving, plus answering the phone. Gregorios' business had remained stagnant for over fifteen years, but while other businesses had gone bankrupt, he had stayed afloat. Romano Shipyard Inc. was next to another boat repair business owned by John O'Connor. He was of Irish origin and had three children. Paul, his eldest son of 19 years, was a hardworking and honest young man. Paul had been dating Gregory's daughter for over three years. Ned and Celian were Mr. O'Connor's other two children. They were 17 and 16 years old. Ned and Celian had a terrible reputation as thieves. The police had arrested both several times for theft and vandalism.

Paul enters Gregorio's business, puts a bag on the table and, with an embarrassed face, asks. "Are these your tools?"

Gregorio opens it and sees that there are several of his tools in the bag.

"They are my tools." Gregorio replies angrily.

"Paul, I love you as a son. I attest to your honesty, and I know my daughter adores you, but your brothers constantly rob and vandalize my place and your father has lost control over them. This must end."

The embarrassed young man replies. "I swear I do my best, but I can't be on them twenty-four hours. I hope that when they turn 18, the police will treat them as adults and things will change."

Paul retreats with his head down without looking at Gregorio's face. Gregorio looks at his daughter and tells her.

"He is a brilliant boy, but if you marry him, we'll be linked to those bandits forever."

Lucia did not answer. She knew her father was right, and the problems were becoming more severe and constant.

That morning, three men entered Gregorio's business. It was obvious one of them was the boss, and the others were his bodyguards.

"Good morning. How can I help you?" Lucia asks.

"My name is Tony, and my friend has given me very good references about your business."

Tony was a mafia lieutenant. He was thirty-five years old, tall, handsome, with black hair and always dressed impeccably. His bodyguards were Dino and Ciano. They were totally different. Dino was tall and stocky build. He was Tony's cousin on his mother's side. Caino was short and chubby, and he has known Tony and Dino since the childhood.

"How glad I am to hear that, sir. Our best advertising is the quality of our work." Lucia replies.

"My yacht has problems. The fuel had water in it. I need to clean the lines and check the engine."

"I don't see any problem. You can bring it today, if you like."

"If I bring it this afternoon, when will it be ready?" Asks Tony.

Lucia starts to write down while asking questions.

"Does the engine shut down when you start it, or does it run for a period and then stop quickly? I am asking this, because it is supposed to have a mechanism designed to shut the engine off if it detects water in the fuel. If you run it like that for a while, there could be major engine damage."

Tony, confused, replies. "I don't know what to tell you."

Lucia smiles and replies. "We will remove the contaminated fuel from the tank and fuel lines. Then we will change the fuel filter, spark plugs and check the engine. If we do not find any other problem, then the day after tomorrow, it should be ready."

"Very well." Tony replies.

Lucia asks. "Will you bring it by the river, or trailer it in?"

"I'll trailer in. I don't want it to damage the engine."

"Perfect, we will open a space in front for you. The parts will be one hundred and two hundred for the labor."

Tony tells her. "I'll give you half now."

"No need, sir. Your word is enough."

At that moment, Gregorio enters and sees Tony with his bodyguards. Gregorio doesn't say a word, but when they leave, he tells his daughter.

"These people are not from around here, much less having a fishing boat."

Lucia replies. "Father, the issue is that they are going to give us work and they are going to pay us. This month has already been quite slow."

O'Connor's two youngest sons were very furious with their brother for spoiling the sale of the stolen tools and were just waiting for an opportunity to take revenge. That afternoon, they saw a luxury yacht enter Gregorio's business. It was rare that type of yachts in those workshops. Ned and Celian looked at each other and saw the perfect time to take revenge.

That afternoon they went to look for buyers for the equipment they were going to steal from the yacht and this time they would get much more than usual. Gregorio worked all day on the yacht so he could deliver it the next day. Ned and Celian waited in their father's business until late at night. Then they broke into Gregorio's business, went to Tony's yacht, and stole all the communications equipment and everything that had value. Then vandalized the yacht to get revenge on Gregorio.

Next morning, Tony arrived at Gregorio's business before Gregorio. About ten minutes later, Gregorio arrives with his daughter to open the business. The young woman greets Tony.

"Good morning, Don Tony. Your yacht is ready. My father worked until late, but he finished it just as he promised you."

They all enter the business and head towards the yacht. Tony sees all the damage to his yacht and yells. "What the fuck is that?"

Gregorio shouts. "Sons of the bitches, they are going to pay for this."

Lucia turns red, covers her face with both hands, and breaks down in tears inconsolably. Tony is moved by Lucia's crying and tells her.

"Don't cry, young lady. I'm not angry at you, but I need an explanation of what's going on."

Gregorio explains what has been happening for a long time with the two youngest sons of Mr. O'Connor, who is the owner of the business next door, and that the police have arrested them, and they are back on the street the next day because they are minors. Gregorio apologized to Tony and promised to pay for the damage. He goes inside the office, picks up the phone to call the police, but Tony takes the phone from him and hangs it up. Tony looks at him and undeterred says.

"You told me that the police can't do anything, so don't bother. I will take my yacht and return it to you when it is a safe place."

Tony takes out three hundred dollars and gives it to Lucia, who was still crying and tells her. "You did your job."

Gregorio did not want to accept the money, but the two men got in the way in an intimidating way. Tony puts his hand on Gregory's shoulder and says.

"I respect the honest man who works. I hate dishonest thieves. They can do this to you, but not to me. I promise you this will never happen again."

Gregorio didn't say a word. He was tired of them and deep down, he would be glad if someone taught them a lesson. Gregorio decided not to work that day and took his daughter home, as she kept crying. On the way home, Gregorio tells Lucia.

"I hope that man gives a good scare to those thieves."

Tony tells his bodyguards. "I want those little bastards gone, so everybody knows they messed with the wrong person, and now I want their business."

That afternoon, Tony's men took a medium size boat to O'Connor's business, claiming it had an electrical problem. Ned and Celian entered the boat to work on the circuit while Paul and his father negotiated the job price at the office away from the boat. The boat had a bomb ready to explode when they turn on the circuit and the boat was carrying several barrels of gasoline. Suddenly, there was an explosion, followed by an intense fire. Paul ran to rescue his brothers from the flames, but the fuel barrels exploded, turning the place into an inferno. Firefighters rushed in to control the fire. They did their best to rescue the youths from the blaze, but none of the three youths survived the fire. Firefighters called Gregorio to the scene in case the fire spread.

Gregorio arrived in a hurry and saw the flames had not crossed into his property. Gregorio saw John O'Connor in an ambulance while the paramedics were working on him. He heard him shouting. "My children! My children!" Suddenly, O'Connor stopped pronouncing words and paramedics gave him CPR, but Mr. O'Connor did not survive. He could not overcome the death of his three sons and died at the scene of a heart attack. Gregorio recognized Tony's men and understood that this had not been an accident. Tony's men looked at Gregorio in an intimidating manner. One of them approaches Gregorio and tells him.

"You are lucky the fire did not affect your business."

Gregorio didn't answer. He just looked at him and walked away to a corner. The man approaches him again and says in a low voice.

"Don Tony always fulfills his promises. You will never have problems with them again."

Gregorio felt guilty about what had happened. He wanted a lesson, but not the death of four people. Gregorio sat on the ground with his hands on his head and wept inconsolably, as if the young men killed in the fire were his own children. He felt guilty about what had happened.

Gregorio arrives home and his wife and daughter run to him, asking what had happened. He breaks down in tears again and tells them of the catastrophe, but he hides the truth of what happened for fear of being implicated. Lucia was heartbroken. This has been a terrible day for her and to this was added the death of her first love and only love of her life. Gregorio locked himself in his room and didn't leave until the next day. Gabriela, Lucia's mother, spent the entire night trying to comfort her daughter.

The next day, Gregorio enters Lucia's room and sees her lying in bed with her mother. Gabriela signals Gregorio not to speak and leaves the room. The girl has finally fallen asleep. She must rest. Gregorio also had a very pale face. He could not assimilate what had happened yet. Gregorio tells his wife.

"I must go check if I have damages in the business. I will return later."

Gabriela hugs him and says. "Take care of yourself. You look terrible."

When Gregorio arrives at his business, he sees Tony waiting for him with his yacht parked in front of the business. Gregorio, enraged, tells him.

"What are you doing here? I don't want to see you anymore in my life."

Tony calmly replies. "I told you; I would come back when this was a safe place. I solved the problem, which, according to you had been going on for years and nobody could do anything. You should be a little more grateful."

"I am not a murderer." Shouted Gregorio.

Tony raises his index finger in front of Gregory's face and says.

"Be careful with what you say, because I have no motive to kill those innocent kids, but you have many motives and even documented by the police. But I didn't come here to convince you of anything. Here is my yacht, and I want it fixed as soon as possible."

Gregorio replies. "I don't have the money to buy everything that needs to be replaced now. I promise to fix it, but not right now."

Tony stands again in front of Gregorio and answers. "I know it, and I also know that it wasn't your fault. I will pay for it, and you will fix it. However, remember that you owe me two favors already."

Gregorio furiously yells at him. "I don't owe you anything."

He hadn't finished speaking when the bodyguard had a gun put under his chin.

The man tells him. "Calm down, no one here has yelled at you."

Tony tells Gregorio. "If you think talking to the police will make you feel better, go right now. I have nothing to worry about, but maybe you can end up being accused of murder."

Tony pulls out a card and gives it to Gregorio. Gregorio, confused, reads it and asks Tony. "Who is Lieutenant Clark?"

"He is in charge of the homicide investigation. Tell him I sent you to give me away."

With that, Gregory understood he was totally at the mercy of Tony. Gregorio returns the card to him and says. "I'll give you a list of what I need to repair your yacht."

Tony replies. "See, it's not that hard to be friends."

Tony stayed in Gregorio's business until he received the list of items needed for the yacht's repair. After thirty minutes, Gregorio hands him a list, and Tony tells him. "Thank you, Gregorio. My men will buy everything you asked for. Please don't hesitate to call me if you forget something else."

On the small island of Ischia, during a frosty morning of 1970, a high-ranking mobster of the organized crime named Don Franco met with an old friend named Vittorio. Vittorio did not belong to organized crime, but he had saved the life of one of its members named Marcelo, who then fled to the United States to save his life. Marcelo settled in the city of Chicago, where he again joined organized crime with ties to the Italian mafia.

Don Franco hugs his friend Vittorio and tells him.
"I contacted Marcelo. He will have a shipyard ready for your son when he arrives in America. I give you my word that no one in the organization will ever bother your son in gratitude for granting us your shipyard and saving Marcelo's life."
Vittorio responds. "You don't know how happy I am for that. My son does not know I have negotiated the legacy of our family. He is a good boy, and he is the only reason I must continue living.

GREGORIO SALES HIS SHIPYARD

Tony had seen a tremendous business opportunity in the late O'Connor burn out shipyard. He thought it would be a strategic place to smuggle any kind of contraband into New Jersey. Tony, through his lawyer, bought the business of the late O'Connor since the wife of the late O'Connor had no money to repair it or pay the back taxes. The city had fined her for not cleaning the premises and repairing it back to code. One day, Tony took advantage of the fact that Gregorio was alone in his business to talk to him.

"Good afternoon, Don Gregorio."

Gregorio looked at Tony, who was dressed impeccably, holding a briefcase in his hand. Gregorio wiped the grease from his hands as he approached the desk. Tony thought Gregorio wiped his hands to greet him with a handshake, but Gregorio left him with his hand outstretched. Tony could not hide the anger he felt at Gregorio's contempt. The bodyguards looked at Tony just waiting for the signal to give him a good lesson and make him understand once and for all who is the boss, but Tony lowered his hand and sarcastically told him.

"All right, since you don't want to be my friend, I'm going to give you another gift to see if I win your valuable friendship."

Tony opens the briefcase and takes out a contract. Gregorio asks him.

"What are those papers?

Tony replies with a smile. "The property of the late O'Connor, just sign here and it will be yours. You'll just have to keep a free space for when I need to fix a boat."

Gregorio categorically replies. "If you think I'm going to make it easier for your contraband to get in, you're totally wrong. I will never lend myself to such things, and I beg you to leave."

Tony takes out other papers from the briefcase, holds them in his hands, and asks Gregorio.

"Which of the two do you want to sign?

"I don't accept your gifts; I won't sign either of them."

Tony laughs. "You are wrong Gregorio, this other is the arrest warrant for the premeditated murder of Ned and Celian O'Connor and the responsibility for the indirect deaths of John and Paul O'Connor. I will be the star witness against you. I can imagine the anguish of your daughter when she learns her father is the murderer of her fiancé."

Tony puts the two documents on Gregorio's desk and tells him.

"Make your decision quickly, because my friend Lieutenant Clark is already parked outside."

Gregorio looks out and sees a police car parked in front of the business, he understands he has no way out. Tony has contact with the police and he does not have the means to fight them. He thinks about the pain he would inflict on his family. Gregorio reads the two documents and sees they are authentic. He has two options: buy O'Connor's business or go to jail.

"I agree to buy, but I don't have the money for such a sum. I've never seen two hundred thousand dollars in my life." Gregorio answers.

Tony laughs and says. "Once again, your great friend comes to the rescue."

Tony takes out a bundle of money of one hundred-dollar bills held by elastic garters and puts them on the table.

"Here is the down payment of ten thousand, which is 5%. That's my contribution to the business. The rest goes on your behalf."

"I have no way to pay the rest." Gregorio answers.

"Yes, you have it. Tomorrow go to the bank of Ireland and ask to talk to Walter Curry. He will wait for you with the loan approval. You only have to put your business as collateral."

Gregorio feels anger and helplessness. He looks at Tony and says. "You had it all planned."

"No, but I never pass up an opportunity to make a good deal. I would have preferred to do business with the O'Connors, but they disrespected me and had to pay for that. Old John and his son Paul were not in the plans, unfortunately they were collateral damage."

Gregory signs the contract, gives it to Tony and says.

"I just hope you respect my family and that my daughter never finds out about this."

Tony returns the contract to Gregorio and responds.

"You should take this contract with the title of your business tomorrow to the bank and don't worry, we are Italians. The family is sacred. Isn't it?"

Tony reaches out and Gregorio sees no other way out than shaking Tony's hand.

Gregorio arrived at his house and during dinner, he tells Gabriela and Lucia he would buy the business of the late O'Connor. Lucia, concerned, replies.

"Father, we are not in a position to expand, that business is destroyed and it's only you and I."

"Well, we will have to get someone who at least can install fences and clean the premises. This is an excellent opportunity. We must take advantage of it."

Gabriela, not pleased at all, tells her husband.

"I think it's time for us to sell and have a more sedentary life. That place has only brought sacrifices and terrible memories. Our daughter has not had a youth. She has spent her youth between boats as if she were a boy. She told me she does not leave because you will be by yourself with no one else to help you."

Gregorio responds. "Let's try. If it doesn't turn out, then we sell and leave New Jersey."

Tony is in his restaurant's luxurious office when he receives a phone call.

"Hello! Tony."

"Hello."

"It's me Marcelo, forgive the annoyance, but I need to ask you a big favor."

Marcelo was one ringleader of the Italian mafia in Chicago and had helped Tony during the beginning of his criminal career. Tony quickly responds.

"You can count on me. I owe you much more."

"I need you to get me a shipyard for a friend. I will pay cash and then send you the name of the future owner. I need that as soon as possible. One more thing, the future owner has no relationship with us, nor can he be bothered by anyone in the organization. He is unaware of this and must stay that way."

"But who is that character?" Tony asks.

"He is the son of the person who saved my life by helping me to escape from the island of Ischia." Marcelo responds.

"Oh! Then you are the one who owes the favor, not me."

"No, this doesn't come from me, this comes from the highest level of the motherland."

Tony thinks Marcelo was joking and tells him.

"I know. I have the place and also the job for him."

Marcelo responds and in a very serious tone.

"This is not a joke. I am telling you that Don Franco himself gave that order. This was an agreement taken at the last meeting held in Ischia between all the families. If you make a mistake like that, it will cost you dearly. I am warning you."

Tony changed his attitude instantly. "Don Marcelo, you can count on me. I would never disobey an order, and I also have the place at the price you are looking for."

"Where is it, and how much does it cost?" Marcelo asks him.

"It's on the Maurice River in New Jersey and it costs four hundred thousand. They are two small shipyards side by side. I have to give two hundred thousand to the owner and the other has a loan at the Bank of Ireland for two hundred thousand."

"Okay, I think it's expensive, but I will not bargain. This must be as soon as possible. Tomorrow, I will send you the name to appear in the contract."

"It will be a pleasure, Don Marcelo."

The next day, Tony went early to Gregorio's business, but Gregorio was gone. Tony immediately went to the Bank of Ireland, hoping to stop the sale of the shipyard, but he was late. Gregorio had signed the loan and was the new owner of the shipyard of the late O'Connor. Gregorio is in the bank parking lot when he sees Tony coming in a hurry. Tony yells.

"Please tell me you haven't signed."

Gregorio replies. "You told me to come early in the morning to signed."

Tony made an angry cry. "Damn!"

"What's the matter? I did what you told me?"

"I know, but now we'll have to do it all over again."

Gregorio looks at him, bewildered. "I don't understand you. What do you mean by that?"

Tony responds authoritatively. "You must sell me back the business."

Gregorio responds, undeterred. "I don't have any problems. That was your idea, not mine."

"Yes, but you will sell me both. I will give you two hundred thousand for yours and I will assume the loan of the second. Tomorrow afternoon, I'll take the contracts to you."

Gregorio angrily replies. "You could keep O'Connor's, but mine is not for sale."

Tony, angrily, replies.

"Look stupid, you have tonight to think about it. You take two hundred and enjoy it or you don't get the two hundred and go to jail. Tomorrow at 11:00 I will pass by your business with the lawyer and the police at the same time and you will choose."

Tony turns around and leaves without saying a word. Gregorio gets into his car and lays his head on the steering wheel, and cries out the great helplessness he fells. He wondered how he had fallen into this trap, where this unscrupulous bandit blackmailed him at will. He composed himself and thought that this was the best thing that could happen. By selling the business, the mafia would have no more interest in him.

Gregorio comes home, hugs his daughter and wife tells them.

"I listened to you. I will not buy O'Connor's business and I will sell ours. We'll start a new life away from here."

Gabriela and Lucia hugged Gregorio. They were happy. They believed that Gregorio finally had heard them, but they did not know the real reason Gregorio was acting like that.

The next day, during breakfast, Gregory tells his daughter.

"You don't need to go to work today. I want you to take your mother out to buy a dress to celebrate tonight."

Gregorio's goal was for his daughter not to witness the encounter with Tony at the shipyard. At 11:00 AM, Gregorio sees Tony arrive and a police patrol car parking in front of his business. Tony, with his two bodyguards, a lawyer with his briefcase and a uniformed police officer with the rank of lieutenant enter Gregorio's business.

Gregorio was pale and visibly nervous. The lawyer puts the contracts on the table and tells him.

"My client informed me you are aware of everything, so I have nothing to say."

The police lieutenant sarcastically says. "Don't worry about me. I'm just on routine patrol, unless you make me do something else."

Gregorio understood what Tony said the day before was totally true. If he did not sign, he would go straight to jail. Gregorio signs without reading or asking questions. That was a fatal mistake. The contract stated that Gregorio was selling both shipyards for two hundred thousand dollars. Tony gives him a check for $200,000 and tells him.

"I am a man of my word; I do not deceive anyone. You only have to keep the business open until the person who will take over the property arrives."

They all left, and Gregorio stayed in the business, going through it with nostalgia, when the phone rang. It was the officer of the Bank of Ireland.

"Don Gregorio, is it true that you sold the business for which you got a loan yesterday morning?"

"Yes, it is true." Gregorio answers.

"Well, then you must pay off the loan first."

"Not Sir, that is a mistake."

The bank representative responds. "I don't think so. In the contract it says that you will give a clean title, so you must pay off the loan. Did you read the contract?"

Gregorio almost fainted. Tony had stolen the fruit of his lifelong labor.

"I don't have that money right now." Gregorio replies.

"You could be sued, and you'll have to pay it, anyway."

"How much do I owe?"

"You asked for a two hundred thousand loan. You gave a down payment of ten thousand. So, you owe one hundred ninety thousand plus two thousand five hundred for the closing cost of the sale. That makes one hundred ninety-two thousand five hundred. Which you must pay this afternoon before 5:00 PM."

Gregorio had no choice but to go to the Bank of Ireland, which accepted the cheque because it was from the same bank of Ireland and received a check for seven thousand five hundred dollars. Gregorio deposits the money into his bank account and keeps quiet about it. He has no courage to tell his wife and daughter what had happened. How could he explain to them he had sold his business for seven thousand five hundred dollars? Gregorio returned home and said he had sold his business for two hundred thousand dollars, and they would continue working until the new owner takes possession of it.

Tony calls Marcelo and tells him.

"Hello Don Marcelo, I already have the shipyards you asked me for. I had to buy both because the owner didn't want to sell just one. It was a fair price of two hundred thousand each. I review the property values with the current market and advise you to do so to clear up any doubts."

Marcelo answers. "I don't distrust you, but I will check everything. I don't want surprises."

Marcelo pauses and tells him. "Tony, I don't know when the future owner will arrive in New Jersey. Can I count on you to pick him up and take him to the shipyard?"

"Don't worry Don Marcelo, just tell me his name, the airline, the flight number and the arrival time. I will pick him up at the airport."

CHAPTER THREE

Alberto Arrives at New Jersey

Six months had passed since the fire at the O'Connor shipyard. Mr. Gregorio and his daughter were still working and had only cleaned the shipyard of the late O'Connor to prevent the city from fine them. Gregorio had aged ten years in the last months. He knew that the truth would come to light and did not know how to deal with it.

Lucia asks. "Father, why are you so depressed if we no longer have to worry about this business and have enough money in the bank?"

Gregorio replies. "It's just that I want to deliver this business as soon as possible."

Tony arrives at Gregorio's business with Alberto and parks in the front. Tony came alone without bodyguards, as Marcelo had ordered him that young Alberto should not have any contact with the mafia. Tony shows him the entrance of the shipyard and takes him to the empty lot that adjoined Gregorio's.

Tony tells Alberto. "This empty lot belongs to you too; you can expand and be one of the largest on the Maurice River."

Gregorio sees Tony is with a young man outside and goes out to talk to them. He doesn't want Tony to come inside, because he fears Tony may expose him in front of his daughter. Gregorio approached while Tony and Alberto were chatting, and they did not notice his presence. Gregorio was curious that Tony was alone, but he was sure that anyone who associated with Tony would be another gangster.

Gregorio interrupts the conversation. "Good morning, Don Tony. I thought you had forgotten about this place."

Tony replies. "I told you I would come back when the new owner arrives."

Gregorio never imagined that the young Alberto would be the new owner. He expected the figure of an advanced age mafioso.

"And when will that man come?

Tony puts his hand on Alberto's shoulder and responds. "Don Gregorio, here he is. This fine young man is the new owner."

Tony proudly taps Alberto's shoulder and says. "WELCOME TO AMERICA."

Gregorio can't believe it and thinks once again Tony is making fun of him, or worse, he is introducing a young man to run a smuggling ring. Gregorio exclaims.

"But he is a child! What experience can this young man have to run a shipyard?"

Alberto, totally unaware of what happened, extends his hand to Gregorio and tells him.

"A great pleasure Don Gregorio. My name is Alberto Rossi, and I am at your service."

Alberto's attitude was so simple and sincere that Gregorio automatically shook his hand, but then he thought he was shaking the hand of a bandit and abruptly removed it as if he had received an electric shock. Alberto looked at him in surprise, but Tony quickly intervened. Unintentionally, Tony and Gregorio had the same purpose. Tony didn't want Gregorio to say anything in front of Alberto, and Gregorio didn't want Tony to say anything in front of Lucia.

Tony tells Alberto. "Please go inside to see the office and the back of the shipyard. We will meet you in a moment."

Alberto responds. "No, I wait for you."

Tony politely tells Alberto. "Please go. I have something personal to say to my friend Gregorio."

Gregorio bit his tongue to keep quiet, but he wanted to finish with Tony once and for all. Alberto apologizes and goes inside the business.

Gregorio said furiously. "What else do you want from me now? You blackmailed me, you stole my business. It is not enough for you?"

"I just need you to stay with him for a month and then you'll never see me again." Tony replies.

Alberto enters the office and sees Lucia organizing the invoices. Lucia's beauty captivated Alberto. Her white complexion, her golden and curly hair, her strawberry-red lips and her emerald green eyes stopped him in his tracks. She looked at him and saw that young Alberto had flushed, that he wanted to talk, but he couldn't. Lucia smiles. She finds it a funny and flattering attitude of the unknown young man. For many months she had not smiled and for a moment she forgot all the sorrows overwhelming her. Lucia seeing that the young man only looked and did not say a word tells him.

"Good morning. Can I help you?"

Alberto tried to speak, but the words did not come out. He had choked and was drowning. He forgot all the English studied. After trying to speak three times, he finally says.

"I only speak Italian. I don't speak English. Do you speak Italian?"

Lucia couldn't hold back the laughter and laughed out loud. Alberto was standing looking at Lucia with a face that looked as if he had been seen naked. He turns around and leaves in a hurry. Lucia tries to call him, but he doesn't even look back. He just hears her saying. "WELCOME TO AMERICA."

Five minutes later, Tony, Gregorio, and Alberto enter the office. Alberto was behind them so as not to be seen by Lucia. The young woman realizes that when her father and Tony walk in, Alberto is practically hiding behind the two.

Gregorio tells Tony. "I have in the back the parts for your yacht that came yesterday. Come on, I will show it to you."

Alberto and Lucia are again alone in the office, and Lucia asks him in Italian.

"Excuse me. What can I do for you?"

Alberto responds with great difficulty in English. "I come for business."

Lucia never expected such an answer, nor did she believe Alberto would be the new owner. She thought it was another entangled Alberto had given. She couldn't hold back and laughed out loud again. Alberto replied in Italian.

"Laugh. Laughter makes you look very beautiful and happy. If I cause that beauty and happiness, then I don't care if you laugh at me."

Alberto sat in a chair and kept silent. Lucia felt praised by Alberto's saying, and it was the first time she had looked at a young man with interest after Paul O'Connor's death. After all, the young man was not ugly. He was tall with black straight hair and was manly. Lucia held back her laughter and from time-to-time crossed glances, but whenever they looked at each other Lucia smiled, until at the end the two laughed as if they were children.

Tony and Gregory enter the office, and Gregorio tells his daughter. "I think I don't need to introduce this young man to you."

Lucia responds. "No, father, the young man came for something, but I don't know what he wants. Maybe he will tell you."

Gregorio responds dryly.

"What he wants, he already told me. He is the new owner of the business."

Lucia felt as if the earth was swallowing her. She turned red, and it was her turn to feel ashamed. Alberto realized the roles had changed and when she looked at him, he smiled mischievously. That incident created a bridge between the two that would unite them for the rest of their lives. Gregorio was so eager for Tony to leave; he didn't even realize what had happened between his daughter and Alberto.

When Tony leaves, Gregorio tells Alberto.

"We will help you for a month, then you will be on your own, so you will have to learn fast because we will not be there for a minute longer. Everything produced so far is mine. What is inside the workshop that is about to end is also mine and I get 50% of what comes tomorrow, because I will not teach you for free."

Gregorio spoke in a derogatory way, which worried Alberto and embarrassed Lucia. Alberto replies.

"I agree with what you propose and believe me, I do not come to offend or bother you. I have no one in this country. I just want to work and follow the legacy of my parents."

Gregorio laughs sarcastically and thinks to himself. "This mobster believes I don't know who he is, or his purpose with this business."

Gregorio speaks again in a derogatory manner.

"You have a copy of the keys on the desk. I will keep a copy until the end of the month. Tomorrow I will come at ten in the morning to finish the repair of the engine in the red boat. You come when you feel like it; you're the owner."

Alberto replies. "I'll be here."

Gregorio attacks again. "Don't worry, you can sleep in the morning; I will steal nothing from here."

Alberto realizes Gregorio is on the offensive and does not understand the reason, so he answers him.

"Don Gregorio, I don't see the reason you treat me this way and I hope that's not the way you are, but if I am here, it's because I have nowhere to go, and this will be my home."

Gregorio thought they would receive contraband that night, and Alberto was trying to hide it, so he didn't even pay attention to what Alberto had told him. Lucia was red as a tomato; she had never seen her father act in such a despotic way. Gregorio tells Lucia as a dictatorial order. "We're leaving"

Lucia replies. "Father, we close in two hours."

Didn't you hear me? I said we are leaving." Gregorio replies.

Alberto is totally confused and looks at Lucia, who is visibly sorry. Gregorio takes his daughter by the arm and almost pulls her out by force. Before getting into the car, Lucia tells her father.

"I forgot something." She knew that this way her father would not object to his daughter re-entering the business. Lucia enters and sees Alberto, who is still stunned.

"I apologize. My father is not like that. I don't know what happened to him. Will you really sleep here?"

"Yes, I don't have anyone, and I just arrived today from Italy."

Lucia tells him. "In the back room, there is a small mattress that I used when there was no work to take a nap."

Alberto thanks her. "If that's your father, he will be a hell of a father-in-law."

Lucia laughs again. She sees Alberto does not hold a grudge against them, since her father had humiliated him and that she herself had made fun of him. Lucia didn't know what to do to amends for the situation and, without thinking about it, gives him a friendly hug and a kiss on the cheek as if they were old friends.

"Everything will go well; we will help you get ahead."

Gregorio angrily asks his daughter. "Why did it take you so long?"

"It's that I lost the handkerchief that my mother gave me, and I thought I had left it in the office. I looked for it everywhere, but I can't find it."

During dinner. Gregorio was very serious and almost didn't want to eat. Gabriela asks him.

"If you're out of the business, then what's bothering you now?"

Lucia also tells him.

"Father, I think you were very unfair to that young man. You treated him terribly."

Gregorio tries to defend himself by saying.

"It hurts me that a business I built with so much sacrifice for so many years will be ruined by falling into the hands of a young man who does not even know how to tighten a nut."

"How do you know he doesn't know about mechanical repairs if you don't know him?" Lucia asks.

"Because that takes years. He is an adventurer who comes like so many others, to look for money the easy way, no matter how."

"Father, you are exaggerating and being unfair by speaking like that about someone you don't even know."

"Lucy, nobody buys two shipyards for $400 thousand dollars and has nowhere to sleep. No one sends a child to another continent alone, with such a large amount of money, where he doesn't know anyone. He has lawyers who buy and do the transactions for him, but he doesn't know anyone or have a roof over his head."

Gregorio's explanations were logical and stopped Alberto's defense.

"Well father, we just have to see him for a month, and we'll be out of there."

Gregorio shows up at the shipyard at 10:00 AM and sees that Alberto is in work clothes and muddy with grease. Alberto sees him coming and tells him.

"Good morning, Don Gregorio. Your engine is already finished."

Alberto thought Gregorio would thank him, but Gregorio swelled his face and angrily told him.

"Young man, I left the engine uncovered so I can work on it. Fixing an engine does not mean covering it without knowing what problem it has. Now I will have double work, thanks to your daring."

Alberto looks at him in bewilderment and replies. "Excuse me, it is because of the time change. I could not sleep, and I worked on it. Why don't you try it and then scold me?"

Gregorio says nothing and passes by Alberto's side, dodging him as if Alberto has an infectious disease. Gregorio goes straight to the boat; he is sure that the engine will not start, and he will be happy to tell Alberto that now the work will be double because of him. Gregorio sees the key is on. He only has to press the start button, but he is afraid that Alberto assembled the engine wrong, and he will damage it even worse. Gregorio was standing with his finger on the button for a long time. There were so many things that could go wrong that he did not dare to press the start button.

Alberto had been looking at Gregorio standing for a while with his finger on the button. He could read on Gregory's face the fear of pressing the start button. Alberto approaches him and says. "Excuse me, Don Gregorio"

Gregorio didn't see him. He was so mad he didn't hear him either. Alberto says to him again in a higher tone. "Allow me, Don Gregorio"

This time, Gregorio heard him. He thought Alberto was coming to look for some tool. Gregorio steps aside, still with his finger on the button. Alberto is standing in front of Gregorio, staring at him. Gregory tells him.

"If something breaks because you dared to repair it without permission, you will be responsible and pay for it."

Alberto puts his right hand on his chin and puts on a frightened face. Gregorio enjoyed the moment; he thought Alberto was terrified and had exposed his mechanical incompetence. The two looked into each other's eyes as if they were in a duel, Gregorio with fire-throwing eyes and a face of revenge, Alberto with a terrified face. Now Alberto drops his hand quickly like one who wants to kill an insect, hitting Gregorio's finger, which was on the start button. Gregorio never expected such a thing from Alberto. He was taken totally by surprise, but even more surprised when he heard the engine start immediately.

Gregorio did not know what to say. His frustration was so great that instead of thanking him, says.

"Who the fuck do you think you are to take such attributions? Also, don't even think that I'm going to pay you for that."

Alberto felt mistreated. He looked at Gregorio and said.

"I do not understand why you treat me this way. I have not disrespected you and even though you have mistreated me, I will not disrespect you. I have not stolen from you or owe you anything. I would like to have a cordial and respectful relationship with you, but I see you do not do your part. Regarding the engine work, I have not asked for anything or wanted anything. Anyway, it was not that difficult."

Gregorio could not answer. Everything Alberto said was true, but he did not want to call him a mafioso for fear that things would get worse, he will have to live with him for a month and then he would disappear. Alberto turned around and left. Gregorio stayed in the back so as not to see Alberto.

About two hours had passed when Gregorio entered the office to get his lunch and saw that Alberto was having a hard time with his poor English with two clients. Gregorio sees one is the owner of the boat that Alberto had fixed, and the other is a known customer to Gregorio. Gregorio listens behind the door when a customer asks.

"Are you new?"

"Yes, sir."

"Where is Gregorio?"

"He's busy right now. What do you need?"

"My boat has an electrical problem."

"I'll fix it, sir."

The customer laughs and responds.

"Do you think I will put my boat in the hands of a brat? Gregorio is the only one who touches my boat."

Gregorio enjoyed what the client said and went out to show off.

"Hello Don Miguel."

"Hello Don Gregorio, so you have a new apprentice."

"No, he's the new owner."

The customers look at each other in surprise, and Gregorio continues.

"I will only work for another month, so I guarantee the quality of the work I do. After that is up to you. If you want to take the risk."

"If you give me your word that you will do the work, I leave my boat."

"I will do it Don Miguel; you can bring it with confidence."

Alberto got angry seeing how Gregorio not only ignored him, but tried to destroy the future of the business.

The other customer asks. "Don Gregorio, is my boat ready? What was the problem?"

"Yes, Don Mario, it is ready, and the engine works perfectly."

"But what was the problem?"

"A little thing, don't worry."

Alberto angrily interrupts. "He can't tell you, because he didn't fix it. I, "THE BRAT" fixed it. As he said, the little things were two worn pistons and some cables that were giving false contacts, so it was a mechanical and electrical problem."

The customers are puzzled. They looked at each other and looked at Gregorio, who was red with a fury he could not hide.

"But you don't have to worry. Don Gregorio supervised my wok, which is the seal of good quality, and if he said it is perfect, you can be sure of that." Alberto looks at Gregorio and says. "Isn't that the case, Don Gregorio?"

Gregorio boils inside. Alberto has put him on the defensive, but he has no other choice.

"Yes, it's true. He did it and I supervised him. You have my guarantee."

Don Miguel says. "In that case, then I will leave my boat."

When the clients leave, Gregorio tells Alberto. "Those two clients are mine. The first one I had already started the work and the second one would never have left his boat in your hands."

Alberto looks at him with bewilderment, shakes his head, and responds. "I will not argue with you about that. The only thing I'm going to ask you is that if you're going to hate me, at least hate me with respect."

Gregorio was a little confused. He didn't expect that answer.

"I don't hate you, I don't hate anyone, I hate actions, not people."

"Could you explain yourself better? Because we don't really know each other." Replies Alberto.

Gregorio stares at him and says. "I don't need to explain what it is very obvious."

Alberto looked very upset. It was his first day, and it was a disaster. Gregorio sees Alberto is going out and asks him. Where are you going?

"I'm going to look for a place to eat. I haven't had breakfast or lunch. Can you recommend one for me?"

"Sorry, I always bring my lunch from home."

Gregorio knew that just one block to the right there was a small cafeteria where many workers had lunch, but he lied. He thought that hurting Alberto was hurting Tony. Alberto headed to the left, and Gregorio knew he wouldn't find a place to eat in ten blocks. When Alberto left, Gregorio immediately went to see Alberto's belongings. Gregorio found inside his clothes an envelope with money. Gregorio counted the money and put everything back so that Alberto would not notice it. Gregorio thought Alberto was the perfect mobster posing as a poor innocent boy. Gregorio realizes Alberto had used his daughter's mattress. He felt angry, took the mattress and put it in the back of his truck to take it away. He would not allow him to use it and he also did not plan to take his daughter to the business anymore for fear that she would discover her father had ties to the mafia.

Two hours later, Alberto returns and finds Gregorio with a client in the office, the client complaining about a terrible job by the late O'Connor.

"Sorry, Don Claudio, but that I bought O'Connor's business does not make me responsible for the bad work he did. That guarantee is not transferable."

"I pay a lot for that work and if I can't get my boat out, I can't work and pay my bills."

Alberto asks the client. What's the problem with your boat?

The customer looks at him, annoyed, and responds to him. "What the fuck do you care about? Don't be curious. Curiosity kills the cat."

Alberto rolls his eyes. Definitely, it was not his day.

"Oh my God, I just was trying to help you. I don't think I offended you."

"I have not asked you for help and I came to talk to the owner of the circus, not to the clown."

Gregorio had enjoyed the moment so much that there was a big smile on his face. Alberto looked at Gregorio and decided that it was enough that he had to be respected.

"Well, believe it or not, you are talking to the owner of the circus, and you should know I am a graduate of the Institute of Naval Mechanics in Naples, and I was one of the first to do underwater welding. When you come next time, you will see my diploma on the wall."

"And who told you I will return to this place?" Answers the customer.

"Well, if you want the problem fixed under Mr. O'Connor's guarantee, bring it."

Claudio changed his expression. The young man had spoken to him clearly and without hesitation, and Gregorio had not said a word. Alberto bluntly asks him.

"So, will you bring it or not?"

"Of course, I bring it, but Gregorio must guarantee the work."

"I will do that work; I guarantee it and it will not cost you anything. Take it or leave it?"

Claudius still does not come out of his amazement. He looks at Gregory as if looking for an answer, but Gregorio also has the same face of amazement.

"Don Claudio, I asked you a question and today is the last day of your guarantee because if you bring it to me tomorrow, I will not accept it. Do you bring it or not?"

"Yes, I will bring it today. The electricity is a disaster. I have already had three short circuits at sea and last time I had to be towed."

"You can bring it today. I will wait for you."

When the client leaves, Gregorio tells him.

"You don't know what you did. Now you will have to do all the wiring. O'Connor never worked the electricity well."

"Well, I guess I will. It is the only way to make myself known and respected because, with your help, I will die of hunger. And speaking of hunger, thanks for sending me almost a mile away. I am sure there must be something closer around here. However, thanks to you, I saw a business opportunity and I already have an idea for ours."

Gregorio responds immediately. "It is not ours, it is yours, although I do not think you really care about it."

"I care a lot more than you, and before I forget, I hope you sleep comfortably on your daughter's mattress tonight."

"I'll take it because she won't come back anymore." Answers Gregorio.

Alberto stopped in his tracks. He needed someone for the papers. He didn't understand taxes or know the system.

"You can't do that to me. You promised Don Tony that you will stay with me for a month."

"Yes, but only me."

"Not both."

"You're wrong."

"Let's call Don Tony to clarify this."

Gregorio felt like grabbing Alberto by the neck. He felt blackmailed by Alberto. He thought Alberto and Tony agreed on everything that had happened. Gregorio took a deep breath and agreed, because he thought if Tony was involved, things would be a lot worse. After all, if Alberto was a mobster, he was low profile, and his daughter would not find out about it.

"Okay, I'll force her to postpone her studies and come to work this month."

During dinner, Gabriela asks Gregorio. How did you do on your first day?

"It's been a crazy day. That business won't last a year."

Lucia asks. "Why?"

"Because that brat takes jobs, he doesn't have a fucking idea about, and he thinks I'm going to be his employee. I am only there to guide him, nothing more."

Gabriela asks. "What do you know about him?"

"Nothing, and everything, because a person who buys two shipyards in cash has lawyers for contracts, a wealthy person picks him up at the airport and takes him to the business as if he was his driver, he has no family or where to live, but he has an envelope with five thousand five thousand dollars in cash. All this means that he must be in something murky."

Gregorio looks at his daughter and says.

"You will go to work with me this month, because I gave my word we would help him, but be very careful and inform me if you see something strange."

"Yes father, do not worry, I will be alert. We cannot get involved in anything illegal."

"If things are like this, Lucy should not go to work anymore." Gabriela replies.

"Don't worry, woman, I will be on the lookout, but I committed myself and I must honor my word. But let's not talk about those things anymore and let's enjoy this delicious dinner."

CHAPTER FOUR

THE SECOND DAY AT WORK

Alberto hoped that his second day would be better. Nothing could be worse than the first. Gregorio and his daughter arrive at the shipyard in the morning and do not find Alberto. Gregorio takes off his hat, starts cleaning his glasses, and tells his daughter.

"I think our boss had enough of playing mechanics."

Lucia looks at the desk and sees nothing. It was just as she left it.

"Father, there is no documentation of what he did yesterday."

"No, and that's not my problem. I'm just visiting. I leave at the end of the month."

"Father, if you promised to guide him, that means in every way, I don't think you're acting in good faith."

Gregorio stopped cleaning his glasses. He did not like at all what his daughter told him.

"I think you're caring too much. This is no longer yours and I think what matters least to that guy is the workshop. Tony brought here him and who knows what kind of business they'll do here."

"I don't understand you father, please explain to me what you mean by that."

"Nothing, Lucy, the less you know better."

Gregorio goes to work on Don Miguel's boat and realizes that Alberto was fast asleep in Claudio's boat. Gregorio enters the boat and turns on the engine on purpose to wake up Alberto. Alberto wakes up with a big scare.

"My God Don Gregorio, you almost killed me."

"It's that how you usually work? Only the rich or the lazy sleep at this mime."

Alberto would not allow another day like yesterday, so he responded immediately.

"You are wrong. Also, sleep those who like me have worked a whole night and those who arrive from another country and are not adjusted to the time change."

"Bravo! One hundred points for that answer." Gregorio replies.

"More than your rating, I need your understanding." Replies Alberto.

Alberto gets out of the boat and goes to the office. The day had started the same as yesterday, but today he was tired and not in an excellent mood. He preferred to put distance between him and Gregorio to avoid a fight. Upon entering the office, he sees Lucia, and it was as if he had seen an angel. Finally, someone to talk to without fighting. He needed to feel he was not totally alone. Lucia saw that Alberto's face change when he saw her, he looks happy as if she was his salvation.

"You cannot imagine how much I needed you yesterday. It was a fatal day. Everyone was against me. No one respects me for being young and they think I know nothing. And my father-in-law is the worst of all."

Lucia smiles and replies. "So, your father-in-law is the worst?"

"Yes, I don't know why he treats me that way, but it will pass."

Lucia looks at him, moves her head, and says.

"Well, get ready, because now it's my turn. Where are yesterday's papers?"

"What papers are you talking about? I swear, I have touched nothing."

Lucia opens a drawer and takes out a folder, puts it on the table and tells him.

"Everything we do here must be documented with receipts attached. That serves as the job guarantee, to pay taxes, to pay salary and in case the government audits us."

Lucia sees Alberto does not know what she is talking about. Lucia takes him by the hand as if he was a child and sits him at the desk.

"You have to master this very well. This business has two parts, one administrative and one operational."

"But Don Gregorio didn't tell me any about of this."

"It's because my father has only dedicated himself to the mechanical part and I to the administrative part."

Alberto puts his hands in a plea and says. "I don't see why this has to change; you can continue to take care of the administrative part."

Lucia laughs. "I did that since I was a kid because it was my father's business."

Alberto kneels. "Please don't leave me alone. This is my dream, but I didn't know it would be so complicated. I need you. I will give you 30%. We will be partners."

Lucia looks at him, puzzled. "Have you gone crazy? I can't accept something like that."

"Please, I just cannot do it in a month. It won't be enough time to learn it."

Lucia responds. "Sorry, my father would never accept it."

Alberto stands and says. "Thank God, the problem is finally solved."

"And how did you solve it?"

"Listen to me, love." Alberto answers.

"What did you say?" Lucia asks emphatically.

"Sorry, I didn't want to offend you. I said it without malice and also from the heart."

"Let's not mix one thing with the other." Lucia answers, but deep down, it didn't bother her at all.

"My father-in-law doesn't have to find out about our agreement. You will carry all the papers and 30% is yours, as simple as that. Also, I have several things in mind, and I need you to do for me. That will produce more revenue. Let's try this month. If at the end of the month you are not satisfied, you can go with your father."

Lucia thought that, if they will work for a month, why not accept it, and it could be a good deal.

"Okay, but my father can't know about this."

"I promise you, my father-in-law won't know anything, but let's start now."

"What do you mean by that?"

Alberto gives her a piece of paper and says. "Take notes."

Lucia takes a pen. "I'm ready."

Alberto replies:

One - Call Don Claudio and tell him that his boat is ready.

Two - Get some construction workers to build a shower.

Three - I need to buy a pickup truck for the business.

Four - Contact an engineer to construct a warehouse on that empty lot.

Five - Put the phone line in my name so I can make international calls.

Six- I need to buy a refrigerator and a stove.

Eight–I need a bed with a mattress.

Nine–I need a dog.

Lucia laughs, and she did not expect such a request and tells him. "Out of all these orders, what you need most urgently is the shower."

Alberto responds. "I know, pleas add to the list everything that is personal hygiene."

"I'll bring that to you tomorrow, but right now I'll start on everything else."

"Thank you, sweetheart. Now I will go to eat something. I will be back in an hour."

"Do you take that long to eat?"

"No, but the cafeteria is far away."

"You can go to the cafeteria on the right, which is only one block away."

Alberto closes his eyes. It was obvious Gregorio had sent him to the farthest place on purpose, but he said nothing and left.

Alberto returns and sees that Lucia had taken two new jobs. Alberto tells her.

"You are very good. See how customers rain on you?"

Gregorio, who was having lunch in a corner, responds.

"Those customers come for me, not for her. She doesn't fix engines."

"It's true, but when you work as a team, it's like a family and the triumph of one is everyone's triumph."

Gregorio stands and stops eating. "I don't see such a team and as far as I know, my family is only three people."

Lucia turns and tells him. "Father, please calm down."

Gregorio does not answer her and walks away.

Gregorio's attitude annoyed Alberto. He would only wait for the right moment for revenge.

Lucia tells Alberto. "I know a person who is selling a pickup truck at a good price. I told him to stop by in an hour and all the other orders are done, only the dog is missing."

"No, the dog is very important to me. You guys leave, and I am left alone without a soul to talk to."

Lucia looked at him with sadness. She saw in Alberto a very simple and humble human being who was alone in a strange country. She tells Alberto.

"I need you to sign me the checks for tomorrow."

"I don't have checks; I only have five thousand dollars in cash."

Lucia looked at him in surprise. "We can't pay in cash. We need checks."

"But I don't have any. Just take the money and if I'm not here, ask your father to look for it. He knows where it is."

Gregorio was surprised. Alberto had noticed that he had checked his belongings, but he tried to deny it, so as not to look bad in front of his daughter. Lucia looked at her father and saw that her father's face was pure embarrassment. Gregorio pretended to be offended and responded.

"I would never check your belongings. You offend me."

Alberto stares at him and answers. "Don't you remember I showed you where the money was in case of an emergency?"

Alberto and Gregorio were looking at each other, and suddenly Gregorio says. "I'm going to work. I will not waste my time in stupidity."

Lucia shakes her head and says. "It doesn't work like that. Without checks, we can't operate."

Alberto answers. "Well, this is your first test. That's an administrative part."

"Understand the business has no checks. I have checks, but not that amount in my account."

"I'll give you the cash, you deposit it into your account and make the checks."

"This is crazy. How are you going to give me that amount of money if you don't even know me?"

"I'd rather say I lost money with a beautiful young woman than with an ugly old woman."

Lucia laughs and says. "You are definitely crazy."

"Yes, and I think you are partly to blame."

Lucia flushed and dodged her gaze, but she was not offended.

Alberto tells Lucia. "I have money in the Bank of Italy, but I don't know where that bank is located, you need to find out where it is, so we can get the money out and open an account in the business name as soon as possible."

"You are asking too much. I am a simple secretary."

"No, you are my right hand. You are part of this business. Fight with me to get ahead together."

Lucia can't believe what she hears. She stares at Alberto and tells him. "I think you want to use me and you're not sincere."

"You're wrong, yes I need you, but never that way. Let's test each other. I asked you for a month, even though I wouldn't mind if it was a lifetime."

Lucia raises her hand and says Stop! "Let's leave it there, a friendship and business are enough."

"Okay, I have to start with something."

Lucia smiles and says. "You are impossible."

Alberto returns with the money and gives it to Lucia. Lucia, surprised, tells him. "And this for what?"

"I already explained to you what to do. I only want one hundred for food expenses. You manage the rest. In my house, my mother managed the money. They say that the money in male hands disappears."

Lucia replies. "I promised to help you and I will fulfill it. I will keep your money, and I will do what you asked me to do."

"You are wrong. I did not give it to you to keep it. I can do that myself. It is for you to manage it and make it grow. It is also your money. Remember that we are testing each other."

"Do you understand that I have to put this money in my account right now in order to make the checks tomorrow?"

"Yes, and you should do it now, before they close the bank."

"What if I disappear with money and you never see me again?"

"I don't care about the money, I could make it back, I could double it, but the part of never see you again would be a catastrophe."

Lucia responds. "I'll go out to the bank right now and bring you some bags of tea to calm down a bit. I think you need them."

Alberto returns to the back of the shipyard and hears that Gregorio was screaming and cursing to relieve his impatience, as he could not solve Don Miguel's boat electrical problem. Alberto approaches Gregorio and asks.

"What's the matter?

Gregorio stands and wipes the sweat from his forehead. His gray hair was in an uproar from scratching his head so much because he could not find the solution.

"Look, boy, I'm not in the mood for stupidity. You better leave me alone."

"Don Gregorio, I can't help you if you don't tell me what the problem is."

Gregorio, about to explode, yells at him. "I am not an electrician, and I did not do this work, so I'm not able to find the problem."

"Don Gregorio, that doesn't answer the question. What's the problem?"

"Fuck! That the damn thing shuts off."

"Did you check the fuses?"

Gregorio looks at him, wanting to throw the clamp he had in his hand and responds ironically.

"Yes, your majesty, they are the right ones, but if I put others of more amperage so that it does not go out, the damn thing catches fire. Is that okay with you?"

Alberto smiles and replies. "You are very upset, and it is very difficult to work electricity like that. Electricity needs patience. It is like putting together a puzzle."

Gregorio couldn't take it anymore and felt that his blood pressure had risen.

"Mr. Genius. Why don't you do it?"

Gregorio pauses for the moment and then finishes his sentence.

"And you can stop talking bullshit."

"Yes, I will work on it tonight. I can't sleep at night, anyway."

"Bravo! Nice way to run away from the problem."

"I don't start now because I'm waiting for a person who is on the way here to sell me a pickup for the business."

Gregorio, visibly frustrated, threw the tools aside.

"Enough for today. I finish tomorrow."

Gregorio enters the office and does not see his daughter and calls her out loud. "Lucia! Lucia!"

Looking at Alberto, he asks. "Where is Lucia?"

"I don't know. She told me she needed to go out."

Gregorio exclaims furiously.

"But how the fuck is she going to leave without telling me anything?"

"She didn't say anything to me either." Alberto replies.

"She doesn't have to tell you anything. Who do you think you are?"

At that very moment, Lucia enters the office and Alberto comes forward to warn her about what is happening.

"Where were you, Lucia? Your father was looking for you, and I didn't know what to tell him, either."

Lucia looks at her father and sees he is very upset.

"But father calm down, nothing has happened."

Gregorio asks her. "Where were you? How dare you go out and not tell me anything? I don't count for anything here anymore?"

Lucia is in trouble; she can't tell her father she went to the bank to deposit Alberto's money into her account. Lucia looks at Alberto and sees that Alberto grimaces like the one who does not know how to get out of this one. Gregorio even angrier tells her. "Don't look at Alberto. I'm the one who's talking to you. I want an answer."

Lucia throws her wallet on the desk and responds angrily.

"Do you want to embarrass me? Fine, I went to buy something. It's something we women need every month. Excuse me if I didn't know that I had to tell you or Alberto."

Alberto opened his eyes. He never thought Lucia could find the right answer in a fraction of a second. Gregorio was speechless and felt embarrassed. He approached his daughter and whispered to her.

"Forgive me daughter, I did not intend to embarrass you, I just went crazy when I didn't see you, it is that if I lose you, I die. I promise it won't happen again. I will wait for you in the car. I need to get out of here. I can't take it anymore."

Alberto and Lucia are alone in the office. Lucia tells Alberto.

"The money is available in the account. Tomorrow I will bring my checkbook to make payments. I hid the toiletries in the front by the left corner so that papa does not see them."

"You are my guardian angel. Without you, I wouldn't know what to do," Alberto replies.

Lucia says. "I must leave. My father is not well. He is very upset, and he has high blood pressure."

"And what happened to the dog?" Alberto asks.

"I found a very nice one, but when I told him you had three days without bathing, he didn't want to come."

"Am I that bad?" Alberto asks.

"If it's not because I see you walking and I hear you talking, I would think you have been dead for three days."

Alberto reddened and lowered his head. "I swear I'm not like this and now you that brought me the toiletries, I can change my appearance. I will be someone else tomorrow."

"I hope so, otherwise no one will want to enter the business," Lucia replies.

Lucia and her father leave, and Alberto works on the boat Gregorio had worked on during the day. After checking it, he finds the problem and leaves it for the other day. Alberto takes the personal hygiene products Lucia brought him, grabs a hose, and takes a good bath, shaves, puts on clean clothes, and lies down to sleep.

The next day, Gregorio and Lucia arrive at the shipyard and see that in the parking lot, there are four vehicles and six people in front of the business. Gregorio gets nervous, thinking the undercover police have a search warrant for the business. Many thoughts pass through his mind, and none are pleasant. Gregorio parks his vehicle but prefers not to leave. Lucia looks at him, puzzled.

"What's the matter, Father? Aren't going to get out?"

"It's that so many people parked in front gives me a bad feeling. We should wait to see what's happening."

"No, father, that must be the engineers who come to give the estimate."

"What estimate? What are you talking about?"

"Father, you don't think Alberto will keep that lot empty forever. He will join the two lots and make a single building with more facilities."

Gregorio, upset, looks at his daughter. He is afraid Lucia will get involved in shady business without knowing it. He is sure Alberto is a member of the organized crime. Gregorio turns on the car's engine and Lucia asks him.

"What is happening, father? Where are you going?"

"Look Lucia, I don't know how you can be so naive and not realize this young man is a bandit. He has nowhere to sleep, but he has money to buy two businesses cash, he has money to expand the business. Tony brought him here from the airport and he was kissing his ass all the time. I am not stupid, and I will not let you get hurt without you realizing it. It is my duty as a father."

Lucia looks at her father in bewilderment.

"Father, you are exaggerating and please, let's get out of the car to see what's going on."

Gregorio threateningly tells Lucia.

"I told you no, and it's my last word."

Lucia saw in her father's face a hatred she had never seen before. Her father had never treated her that way.

"Father, those men are waiting for me. They were told to come here this morning. I must see them and if it is something else, we will leave."

"I said you're not going, and that's it, or you will not respect my orders." Yells Gregorio.

Lucia, in an act of rebellion never seen before and with total determination, responds.

"Well, I am getting out and if you start the engine, I will open the door and jump out."

Gregorio was surprised. His daughter has never contradicted him. He feels he is losing all the battles. Gregorio turned off the engine and hit the steering wheel with both hands while screaming.

"Damn Tony, damn Alberto, damn everyone."

Lucia couldn't believe her eyes. She doesn't understand what is happening to her father, but she decides she would find out later. She gets out of the car and walks toward the entrance of the business. Gregorio closes his eyes and clenches his fists, trying to control his fury. Gregorio gets out of the car and walks towards the business, almost dragging his feet. Lucia is nervous, her father's attitude is not normal, nor it is usual for so many people to be in business so early and to that is added that Alberto had not opened the door.

"Good morning. Sorry for the delay. Who comes from the construction company?"

A middle-aged man comes forward and responds.

"Good morning. My name is Robert, and these two gentlemen are my companions. We have an appointment early in the morning, but no one is inside because we knocked many times and very hard. We were already leaving."

"I apologize again. The owner must be inside. I don't know what has happened."

Lucia looks at the other three and asks them. "How can I help you?"

A young boy comes forward and responds.

"My name is Daniel and I'm looking for a job."

"Well, we will talk to the owner about that as soon as we enter."

The other two turned out to be customers who wanted an estimate for their respective boats. Lucia pounds on the door but gets no answer. Lucia turns around and sees that her father is still halfway there. Lucia yells at her father.

"Quick, father the keys. Something is not right. Alberto does not respond."

When Gregorio heard what his daughter said, he stopped in his tracks. Nothing good must have happened. He didn't want to open the door; he didn't want his daughter to see a horrible scene. Lucia ran to him and asked for the keys. Gregorio sees his daughter's worried face and felt mixed feelings. On the one hand, he felt more anger, but he also felt sorry for his daughter. Gregorio tells his daughter. "You wait here; I will open the door."

Gregorio opens the door, turns on the lights, and sees Alberto's feet on the ground protruding from behind the desk. Lucia screams.

"My God! What happened?"

Gregorio, thinking Alberto is dead, stops his daughter, hugs her, and tells her.

"Sorry, Lucy, you should not see this. It is not pleasant at all."

Lucia hugs her father and cries inconsolably, screaming.

"He's dead. No, no, no, he can't be dead."

When the men outside heard Lucia's screams, they rushed in to render aid. When the young Dany runs inside, collides with a chair and falls, making a great rumble. Alberto wakes up to Lucia's screams and Dany's rumble. He stands scared. He doesn't know what is happening when he sees so many people in the office. Engineer Robert helps stand Dany up from the floor and asks.

"Is this the dead one?"

There is a moment of silence. Everyone is motionless. Only Alberto moves his head, looking at everyone, expecting for someone to explain what had happened. Lucia, still crying, takes a jug of water that is on the desk and throws it at Alberto.

Alberto screams. "What is going on? Have you all gone crazy?"

"You almost killed us from the fright, we thought something bad had happened to you." Lucia replies.

"I finally could sleep. You know I haven't slept for several days."

Gregorio could not help his displeasure; he had not liked his daughter had shown so much concern for Alberto. Lucia still held herself, hugging her father between sobs.

Robert asks Lucia. "Where is the owner, please? "I've wasted enough time already."

Gregorio reluctantly points to Alberto. "He is the owner."

Dany wastes no time. "Sir, I came to see if."

Lucia lets go of her father and tells Dany.

"You sit down and wait. I can't take care of you right now."

"Excuse me, I thought you told me I had to talk to the owner." Dany replies.

"Yes, but now I am telling you to wait. If you don't like it, you can leave."

Lucia was upset. Everyone was looking at her, but not even her father said a word. Lucia, with an authoritarian character which she had never exhibited before, says.

"Enough dramas for today. The dead man is alive, so let's not waste any more time."

Lucia gives orders as if she was the owner of the business. It was the only way she found to calm her nerves.

"Father, please attend to these two gentlemen. Alberto, you come with me to talk to the engineers. You Dany, I change my mind, you work right now, dry the water on the desk and my father will find something for you to do in the yard."

Gregorio looks at her, bewildered, and says.

"But what the hell is wrong with you.? Since when you are the owner and give orders here?"

Lucia ignores and tells Robert. "Follow me, please."

Robert and the other two workers follow her, and Gregorio still does not come out of his amazement. Alberto puts his hand on Gregorio's shoulder and says in a low voice and almost begging him.

"Understand her, please. She is very nervous. Help us with these two gentlemen and give the boy something to do."

It was the first time that Gregorio did not contradict Alberto, but he only did it for Lucia. Gregorio looks at Dany and vents his rage against him.

"What are you doing standing there? Didn't she tell you to dry the desk?"

"Yes, sir." He quickly picks up a cloth that was on the floor and starts drying the desk.

"Excuse me gentlemen, today is a day that I would have preferred to stay at home." Says Gregorio.

"Ho no, on the contrary, I think it has been more entertaining than the theater." One client responds. His comment was so timely and witty that even Gregorio laughed.

Robert, the engineer, looks at the fenced lot next to the business and asks Alberto.

"Tell me what you have in mind?"

Alberto looks at Lucia and says.

"We want to repair the two docks, make a building that joins this one, and I want a cafeteria restaurant on the second floor. I also want a spacious room with a full bathroom and a small kitchen. Finally, I want a very large billboard to put on a neon advertisement which can be seen from far away."

Alberto looks at Lucia again and asks.

"Are you okay with that, Luci?"

Lucia still looks at him with rage. It was the first time he called her Luci, but she did not want to fight so as not to add more problems to the day. She only responded sarcastically. "Yes, sweety."

Lucia's sarcasm produced a big smile on Alberto that infected Lucia and the two ended up smiling. The engineer tells them.

"I will start by making the blueprints. If you approve it, then I will take it to the city hall to get the permits to start the work. This is not cheap work, especially when the two docks must be done again, and they should pass a rigorous inspection."

Lucia responds. "I understand. Let's go to the office to write the contract."

As soon as they enter the office, Gregorio asks Alberto.

"Did you finish last night with the electrical work on the boat?

"No, I couldn't."

"Beautiful! Aren't you the one who knows everything and told me you were going to do it? What do I tell the owner when he calls me?"

Gregorio responds with satisfaction, thinking that Alberto did not know how to fix the problem.

"Don Gregorio, the problem is that the wires they put on it are not the right ones. It needs a thicker wire. That is the reason it heats, and the fuses cut the electricity to avoid a fire. I looked, but we don't have the right wire. I need to buy it today."

Gregorio realized Alberto had found the problem that he could not find, but he did not give up and responded.

"I would have found the problem if you hadn't gotten in the way, and now we lost another day and have to place the order in New York."

"Why New York? There is nothing closer?

"No, and now we will have the boat tucked in the dock for a week." Gregory replies, angry.

Alberto turns around and says to Robert.

"Good thing you haven't started yet. There is a change of plans."

Lucia and Robert look at him, intrigued.

"What's wrong? What are you talking about?" Lucia's question.

"It's that your father gave me a great idea." Alberto replies.

Gregorio heard what Alberto said, closed his eyes, and took a deep breath. He could not avoid his anger against Alberto.

"Instead of making a building that join this one, we will make a warehouse to sell everything related to the marine supply, so we will not have to wait to make a repair and we will become suppliers, everything else remains the same including the cafeteria on second floor."

Alberto looks at Gregorio and tells him.

"Don Gregorio, you are a genius. Thank you for such advice. You deserve a hug."

"If you want to be funny in front of people, look for someone else. I'm not for your games or disrespect." Gregorio, rudely, responds.

The engineer responds. "That will make the job easier. We only need 25% to get started."

"No problem. I will give you the check." Alberto answers with a smile.

Robert immediately flashed his eyes and turned to Lucia. Lucia says.

"No, sir, do not even think about it. You bring the blueprints. If we approve it, we will pay for it. We will pay for all the city permits and so we will pay you according to the finished work."

Alberto tells Lucia. "But the gentleman said."

Lucia won't let him finish the sentence. "The engineer will get paid for work done, not for the work he will do."

Robert replies. "Young lady, I must invest money and time in your project. It's not fair."

"Look sir, if you bring your boat here, you pay for it after it is fixed, and we put time and parts that we buy with our money. Why, if we do that, you can't?" Lucia responds firmly.

"I don't work like that."

"Well, neither do I, so we can't make a deal. Have a good day." Lucia replies.

Everyone was quiet, watching the duel between Lucia and the engineer. Gregorio was proud to see his daughter had such a talent, but it annoyed him that Lucia behaved like the owner of the business and defended Alberto's interests. The engineer looked at Alberto, who was with his mouth open and totally amazed.

"I thought you were the owner and decided."

"Yes, I am the owner, but she decides in this case. If she wants it that way, that's the way it will be, or we will look for another engineer."

The engineer moves his head, looks at Gregorio, who tells him.

"Don't look at me. I have nothing to do with this business."

The engineer understands Lucia will not give in, that they will not give him the job.

"I understand you are a young couple, and you are fighting very hard for your money. I admire that, and I will accept it just to help you."

Those words were like a bomb for Gregory, who turns red, raises his right hand in a sign of stop and screams.

"Wait a minute, make no mistake. My daughter is not the wife of that guy. She does not have such poor taste, nor will I allow her to lower herself to such a level."

The engineer understood it was better to shut up, sign the contract and get out of there as soon as possible.

When they are alone, Gregorio tells Lucia and Alberto.

"Now you're going to explain to me what's happening here. Why are you acting like if you were the owner?"

"Father, I realized they could scam him, and I didn't allow it. You would have done the same too."

"I'm not that stupid, and I wasn't born yesterday. What you are saying is very far from the truth. Be very careful with what you are doing."

Gregorio looks at Alberto and says.

"And you don't play with fire, because you are going to get burned."

No one said a word. The situation was so tense that the three of them were silent, but Dany comes in holding a broom in his hand asks Gregorio.

"Don Gregorio, I am done. What do I do now?"

Gregorio screams. "Look boy, sweep the sea, but get out of my sight."

"Father, calm down, please. You are going to have a heart attack."

"Yes, and you both will be to blame. This is good enough for today. We are leaving." Shouts Gregorio.

Lucia looks at Alberto, who tells her.

"I think it will be better for you to go home with your father. Tomorrow is another day. I hope it is much calmer."

CHAPTER FIVE

Gregorio Suffers A Heart Attack

The next few days were apparently calm. Gregorio did not speak, and when he did, it was to contradict Alberto or to scold his daughter. He only established a cordial relationship with Dany, perhaps because he was almost a child and not related to Alberto. Gregorio was convinced Alberto was living in the shipyard to supervise the receiving of some kind of contraband at night, but he could not decipher what it was. Lucia and Alberto had developed a cordial friendship, and Alberto did not take a step without consulting her. Lucia inadvertently felt in control, not only of the business, but also of Alberto.

Lucia approaches Alberto and tells him.

"You bought the truck from my friend, but you have not moved it for a week. It will get damage if you don't use it."

Gregory does not waste the opportunity and says.

"That only happens when the money comes in easily and you don't know what to do with it."

"Neither one Don Gregorio. I bought it because I need it for business."

Gregory returns with sarcasm.

"You need it so much; you have not moved for a week."

"I don't move it because I don't know how to drive, and I don't have a driver license. I'm from an island where a motorcycle is enough. I did not think that we would be that busy. I thought I would have time to learn. I don't know how much work you had before, but I am up to my neck."

Gregory does not believe a word of what Alberto is saying. He approaches him and says in a low voice.

"You don't fool me. Either you are the smartest bandit there is or the stupidest, and so far, you haven't shown me any intelligence."

Alberto looks at him seriously. He is upset. "I treat you with respect, but you offend me constantly."

Gregory stands in front of Alberto and says in a low but defiant voice.

"I do not intend to offend you, I am only honest with you. I do not lie, but don't worry, soon you will not see me again. Remember that the agreement is thirty days, and it is coming soon. We will rest from each other at last."

They both stared at each other with fire in their gazes. Gregorio continues to walk forward and with his shoulder intentionally collides with Alberto provoking him, his intention was for Alberto to lose control and hit him and that way he would put Lucia against him. Alberto closes his fists. He wants to punch Gregorio. He had never been provoked and humiliated in such a way, but he remembers his father's advice: "Never give in to provocations, hang on to your principles and respond politely. You will see that no matter how painful it might be, the victory will be yours."

Gregorio expected an answer from Alberto, but seeing that Alberto had not reacted, he turned around and looked at him defiantly, sees that Alberto had his eyes closed and tried once again to provoke him.

"Why do you clench your fists if you don't have balls to use?"

Those words hurt Alberto, who steps forward and almost lost control, but he stops, turns around and leaves. Gregorio was impressed. He tried everything, but he couldn't get Alberto to hit him.

Gregorio enters the office and sees Robert, the engineer, with Lucia.

Robert puts some blueprints on the desk and says.

"These are the blueprints you chose. The city council has already approved them and here are the building permits. It all adds up to three thousand one hundred dollars."

Lucia takes out the checkbook and makes a check, saves the blueprints, and asks the engineer.

"What else do you need from us?"

"Nothing, just to allow us to keep the construction equipment in the parking lot. We start tomorrow."

Gregorio is in total bewilderment, still not coming out of the amazement of what he had witnessed. When the engineer leaves, Gregorio, with a rage about to burst, tells Lucia.

"Since when the fuck, you can sing checks for three thousand one hundred dollars as if you were the owner? What the fuck is going on here?"

"Father, calm down. Alberto put me on the account so that I could manage the accounts and make the checks, because he still does not understand those things."

"Do I look like an idiot? Do you think I'm going to believe that? No one gives control of such a sum of money without asking for anything in return."

Gregorio points his finger at her and says threateningly. "Careful with what you do. You are not just anybody."

Lucia, offended, responds. "Wait a minute father, you respect me,"

"In that case, give yourself some respect first, then we will see. Thank God that in a week we are leaving, and you will not stay here working with that asshole."

Lucia sees her father is totally out of control and decides not to respond and leaves to look for Alberto. On the way, she asks Dany. "Where is Alberto?"

"I don't know what's wrong with him. He is standing at the end of the pier looking out to sea."

Lucia asks Dany. "Did my father and Alberto argue?"

"I don't want to get involved. Please don't ask me."

Lucia looks at Dany, who looks nervous. "Don't worry, this won't come out of here."

"Yes, your father was very rude to him and disrespected him, but Alberto did not answer back."

Lucia gives Dany a hug. "Thank you, Dany. I don't know what's wrong with my father. He is not like that."

"I know. He treats me like a son."

Lucia sees Alberto standing at the end of the pier, looking at the sea. Alberto was so furious he didn't hear her approaching. Alberto hears Lucia calling him and turns to answer. Lucia sees Alberto has tears in his eyes. She knows they are the product of her father's mistreatment and can't help but feel embarrassed and guilty.

"Sorry Alberto, believe me, I'm sorry and I apologize a thousand times. I don't understand what happened to my father. I don't recognize him myself." Says Lucia.

"I don't know what you're talking about. I have had no problems with your father. I am the one that should apologize to you for not being with the engineer." Alberto answers.

Lucia looks at him and replies in a sweet tone. "You are a nice person. You do not deserve such treatment. I will not allow it."

Lucia turns around to complain to her father, but Alberto stopped her and takes her by the arm.

"No, please, don't do it. I don't want you and your father to fight because of me."

"It's not your fault, and I will not allow that injustice." Lucia replies.

"No, please, I ask you. He says that in a week he is not coming anymore. I can handle it, I promise you, but there is something you can do for me, I would thank you from the bottom of my heart."

Lucia, with watered eyes, replies.

"Okay, but if something like this happens again in front of me, don't expect me to be quiet. Now tell me. What do you need?"

"I need you to take me to church."

Alberto's request took Lucia by surprise. "I didn't know you were religious."

"For as long as I can remember, I have been going to church every Sunday with my parents. Only God can give me the strength to endure your father and he takes care of me through you, who are my guardian angel."

Lucia is silent for a minute and responds. "I promise you this Sunday, I'll take you to church, but now let's talk about business. I was doing the paperwork then I realized in three days is the end of the month. Do you want me to close the month or extend it until the fourth, which is the day that my father is leaving?"

"No, I prefer you close it on the last day of the month, so you can compare it with the previous months and remember that you own 30% and such should be your check."

Lucia asks. "Are you sure of what you are saying? You might regret it later."

"No, we already talked about it. We put ourselves to the test, and you did a great job."

The next two days passed with a tense calm. Alberto stayed away from Gregorio and used Dany to communicate with him. The boy had won the affection of all. He had shown honesty, punctuality, and a great desire to learn. On the third day, the calm ended when Gregorio saw Lucia taking Alberto's pickup truck keys.

"Where do you plan to go with that vehicle?" Gregorio asked emphatically.

"I'll go home with it; it's been standing for more than a week." Lucia replies.

Gregorio clutches his eyes and takes off his cap. He squeezes the cap to calm his fury. And that was only the beginning.

"Monday marks the month we promised to be here. I will come to turn the keys over to him and you do not need to come. Finally, in two hours, our commitment is over."

Lucia doesn't answer him, but she doesn't return the keys either. Gregorio realizes Lucia does not return the keys, but thinks he has been clear enough with his daughter. Alberto and Daniel enter the office and Gregorio leaves the office as if he had seen the devil. Lucia tells Dany.

"I need you to entertain my father for a while. Do your best to keep him busy for at least fifteen minutes."

Dany scratches his head. "He's very upset. I know his face. I don't know how long he can hold him."

The boy turns around and goes to find Gregorio. Lucia takes the papers out of the drawer and tells Alberto.

"I just closed the month. Here are the numbers for you to review."

"If you did it yourself, I don't have to check anything. Just tell me how we come out." Alberto answers.

"We started badly the first week, but the other three were amazing. We had a net profit of one thousand."

Alberto opens his mouth; he can't believe it. Did you deduct expenses, your father's share, and Dany's salary?

"Yes, that's already deducted."

Alberto is happy, and Lucia adds to that happiness. Alberto opens his arms and says.

"We must celebrate this; I knew that with your help, we will move forward."

Alberto gives a big hug to Lucia, who does not put up resistance because she knows it is a hug of joy.

"How do you plan to celebrate it?" Lucia questions.

"Well, we will go to church on Sunday to thank God and then we will go to the restaurant of your choice. I would also like you to invite your mother and father."

"I promised to take you to church on Sunday. The other thing is very difficult. I don't think my father will accept it and my mother only does what my father says." Lucia replies.

Lucia puts a blank check on the desk and says.

"Now it's your turn to pay my salary."

Alberto laughs and replies. "You can sign your own checks. That's not my job. That is the reason you get paid 30% of the profits."

Lucia reddens and responds. "I can't accept that. It is three hundred dollars."

"I thought we had a deal, but I see you don't want to fulfill it. In that case, I will sign your check, but this will be the last check I sign for you."

Lucia is perplexed. She thinks Alberto is upset but keeps quiet and gives the checkbook to Alberto. He takes the checkbook, writes a new check, folds it, and gives it to her.

"You forced me to do it. Anyway, nothing changes for me."

Lucia takes the check and opens it and sees that the figure is three hundred and fifty.

"Have you gone crazy? I meant that three hundred was a lot and now you give me more. I've never made so much money in my life."

"I only gave you what you deserve. Without you, nothing would have been possible. Now you own 35% of the business and 100% of my heart."

Lucia was surprised. She did not think Alberto would fulfill his promise to include her as owner. She had worked the month with him as if the business were hers, but she had doubts Alberto was going to keep his word. Now he went up 5% more. Lucia, full of joy, runs to Alberto, hugs him, and kisses on the cheek. Lucia didn't notice that her father was entering the office and saw her run to Alberto, hugging him and giving him a kiss on the cheek.

"Lucia!!!!!!" Gregorio screams out loud.

"You are shameless. How dare you?"

Lucia jumped back like a spring. "Father, it is not what you think. We are just celebrating the closing of the month, which has been great."

Lucia takes out two checks and says. "Here's Dany's salary."

She gives the check to Dany. This was the first check he received in his life. Daniel, out of joy, gives Lucia a hug and Lucia kisses him back.

"You have earned it, Dany." She responds.

Lucia extends her hand and says.

"Look, father, here is your check for all the jobs that went on your name even though many of then you did not do it."

Gregorio takes the check and doesn't even look at it.

"And how much is your check, if I may know?"

"My check is three hundred and fifty." Proud Lucia answers.

Gregorio was even more enraged. He had never paid his daughter so much. He thought it was easy money that came to Alberto for dirty business he did at night. Gregorio broke his check into pieces.

"Look what I do with my check. I don't need it and I prefer to ask for alms before accepting it, but you have set a price for yourself. You are worth three hundred and fifty dollars. I am ashamed of what I see here."

Lucia was enraged. She couldn't believe her father could refer to her like that.

"Respect me, father, I respect you." How dare you talk about me in that way?"

Alberto, who had always remained on the sidelines so as not to worsen the situation, intervenes.

"Don Gregorio, I have allowed you to mistreat me, offend me, provoke me and humiliate me without provocation, but I will not allow you to offend Lucia in front of me, that line you cannot cross in front of me. I want you to know that she is indispensable in this business and has earned every penny of her salary. Maybe you don't give her the credit she deserves, but I do. That's why she owns 35% of the business."

Gregorio loses control completely, stands in front of Alberto, and shouts in his face.

"My daughter is not for sale, miserable thief. You have already disgraced my life, but I will not allow my daughter to be harmed."

Gregorio raises his hand and slaps Alberto in the face with all his strength. Alberto did not defend himself and responded by looking him in the eye firmly.

"You can hit me if that satisfies you, but don't you dear to touch my Lucia."

Those words had a significant effect on Lucia. She felt protected and respected by that young man who was also giving a lesson in chivalry to her father, but in Gregorio, they were like pouring gasoline on the fire. Gregorio slapped Alberto two more times as he stood in front of Gregorio without answering back. Gregorio's anger was so great that his eyes became cloudy, and he felt a great pain in his chest. Gregorio put his left hand on his chest and held on to a chair with his right hand. Lucia realized instantly that her father was not well and ran towards him. Alberto tried to hold him, but Gregorio was breathless and almost unable to speak said.

"Don't touch me. You are a curse. This is all your fault."

Gregorio fell to the ground and lost consciousness. Lucia lost control and cried. She hugged Dany so tied that Dany's eyes were about to pop out.

"Please, you are hurting me." Dany tells her.

Alberto grabs her by the arms and tells her.

"Don't lose control please, call an ambulance."

But Lucia's nerves betrayed her, and she couldn't stop crying. Alberto had to use force to separate Lucia from Dany and then yelled at Dany.

"What are you waiting for? Call an ambulance."

Daniel reacts and calls the ambulance. Alberto unbuttons Gregorio's pants and shirt, fans air on Gregorio's face, and wets his forehead with a damp cloth. For an eternal fifteen minutes, Alberto tried to help Gregorio while Lucia cried, hugging Dany again.

The ambulance arrived and quickly worked on Gregorio, who was in critical condition. One paramedic asks Alberto.

"Is it your father?"

"Yes." Alberto replies.

"Do you have health insurance?" Alberto took at Lucia, waiting for her to respond, but Lucia did not react.

Alberto grabs Lucia by the arm and shakes to make her react.

"We need to know which hospital to take him and what type of health insurance he has."

Lucia knew her father did not have health insurance, but she thought her father had 200 thousand dollars in the bank for the sale of the business. Gregorio never told them the truth that there were only 8 thousand dollars left in the bank. Lucia responds firmly.

"We don't have insurance. We will pay in cash. Please take him to the best hospital."

Alberto takes the keys to the business out of Gregorio's pants and throws them to Dany.

"Take over of the business. We are going to the hospital."

Lucia and Alberto followed the ambulance to the hospital. Gregorio was transported to the best cardiology hospital in the area. Gregorio was immediately admitted, while Lucia and Alberto went to the admission department. Lucia felt guilty about what had happened. After filling out the admission papers, the young nurse asks Alberto.

"Is she your wife?"

Alberto responds. "She is my sister and my mother, but she is not my wife yet."

The admissions clerk hears Alberto's answer and laughs.

"This boy is smart; he knows after the day he gets married things change radically."

Everyone laughs except Alberto and Lucia, Alberto for not understanding and Lucia for not listening.

The admission secretary tells Alberto.

"Transportation and admission to intensive care for three days will be three thousand."

"But why three days if he just came in?" Alberto asks.

"He won't come out in three days. Most likely it's much longer."

Alberto tells Lucia. "Please write a check for three thousand dollars."

"I don't have that much money; I have to take it out of my father's account." Lucia replies.

"Sorry, lady, but you must pay before you leave."

Alberto responds. "Don't worry, I will pay the bill."

Alberto tells Lucia. "Make a check from the business account. There are enough funds there."

Lucia takes out the checkbook and writes the check and tells Alberto.

"You are a wonderful human being. I don't understand why my father hates you so much."

"It's father's jealousy, I understand. I just hope that one day he will understand that no one is going to take care of his daughter better than me. Now you must take a taxi and go home to inform your mother about what is happening."

"I can't leave my father alone." Lucia replies.

"He won't be alone; I'll stay here with him. Then you both drive to the business. Tell your mother to drive your father's vehicle and you keep the business' pickup truck so both of you will have transportation."

Lucia didn't know how to thank Alberto; she hugged him tightly and says.

"Don't abandon me. I need you more than you can imagine."

"I repeat to you once again, you own 35% of my business and 100% of my heart."

Lucia hugs him again and when she separates from him, she realizes her dress is stained with engine grease as if she was just another mechanic.

Lucia arrives home to break the bad news to her mother, but as soon as Gabriela saw Lucia's face, she knew something bad had happened to Gregorio. They both burst into tears and hugged. Gabriela tells her daughter.

"I know something was going on. He's not the same since he sold the business, but no matter how hard I try, I can't get anything out of him. I just know he hates the new owner and blames him for his misfortune, but he doesn't tell me why or what his misfortune is."

Lucia replies. "At least with you he speaks. Now I am learning about this, because with me he does not even speak, mistreats and offends me."

"Why hadn't you told me that, Lucy?"

"Because I do not want to bring the problem to the house. All I know is that he hates Alberto, yells at him, offends him and even hits him."

"What did you say? He hits him?"

"Yes mother, and Alberto has never disrespected him. Just today, before he got his heart attack, he offended me, and he hit Alberto in front of me three times in the face."

"What did he tell you that offended you?"

"He basically called me a prostitute, just because Alberto and I worked hard to raise the business. He wants the business to be ruined. The first week was a terrible week; then Alberto offered me 30% of the business if I worked with him. I accepted, and we worked very hard for the rest of the month. Today we close the month with record earnings."

"But, daughter! How can you be so naïve? Do you think Alberto will give you 30% of the business? That's the reason your father was angry. He doesn't want anybody to take advantage of his daughter."

"You are right. Mother Alberto did not keep his word; he did not give me 30%."

"It was to be expected, Lucia. Only a fool would believe that."

"He gave me 35% and we have many plans for the future."

Gabriela, surprised, thinks for a moment and says.

"There is something here that does not fit. I cannot believe that Alberto gives you 35% with nothing in return."

"Mother, you are going to offend me too; I have had enough today."

Gabriela moves her head and responds. "Let's not talk about it anymore.

It's not the right time. We have to go see your father."

Gabriela puts a plate of food on the table and tells her daughter.

"You must eat before you go out. You look pale."

"Yes mom, I have only had breakfast and the night will be long. We have to go to the business to get the pickup truck and then go to the hospital."

Gabriela hugs her daughter.

"Eat and bathe, you have more grease in your clothes than mechanics."

Lucia takes a bath, eats, and tells her mother. "Mother, we should bring a plate of food to Alberto. He didn't have lunch either and must be starving."

Lucia saw that her mother did not like that she asked for a plate of food for Alberto.

"Surely he has already eaten. Or he doesn't eat when you are not there?" Gabriela replies.

"He's in the hospital with dad, he stayed there taking care of him."

"He shouldn't be there; he knows your father hates him and is partially to blame for this problem." Gabriela responds somewhat angrily.

Lucia looks at her mother with tears in her eyes.

"No mother, please no. Are you also going to turn against Alberto without ever having seen him?"

"I don't need to see him. You have told me your father hates him and that all this is related to him."

Lucia responds in a higher tone.

"Just because my father hates him doesn't mean he hates my father. Right now, he's in the hospital taking care of him."

"Well, he shouldn't be there if your father didn't want to see him when he was healthy, let alone see him now that he's sick."

"If Alberto had not been there and paid the three thousand dollars for the admission, maybe dad......"

"Shut up! Don't dare to even say such a thing. Your father is strong, and he will survive this bad time." Gabriela responds as a scolding.

"Okay mother, it's just that this is the first time I have seen you bothered to give someone a plate of food." Lucia replies and leaves for her room.

Gabriela is confused and struggles with her mixed feelings. On the one hand, her loyalty to her husband turns her against Alberto, but on the other she has no evidence to judge Alberto. She reluctantly enters the kitchen and prepares a dish to take to Alberto. Lucia comes out of her room and sees her mother has a bag with food and a drink. She approaches her mother, hugs her and tells her.

"Thank you, mom, there is nothing more beautiful than being grateful."

Upon arriving at the business, Lucia gives Gregorio's car keys to her mother. Gabriela thought her daughter would take Alberto's car so he could return. The two women drove to the hospital and then went to the Gregorio's room. When they arrived, they saw Alberto talking to the doctor. They both ran towards him. Gabriela takes the doctor by the arm, and crying, asks.

"How is my husband, doctor?"

The doctor tries to calm her down and responds. "Relax lady, I just explained to your son."

Gabriela responds, almost screaming. "He is not my son."

The doctor, with a shocked face, responds.

"Excuse me, is that since the young man has been all the time inquiring about the patient's condition and I have seen him so worried, I thought he was his father? I did not want to offend you."

Gabriela understands she has made a mistake.

"No, please, you excuse me. I'm very nervous and I don't even know what I'm saying."

Gabriela looks at her daughter, who is totally embarrassed. She takes her by the hand and says.

"I am sorry, Lucy." Then she looks at Alberto, who is with his head down and visibly embarrassed. "Excuse me, young man, don't take it as an offense. Forgive me."

"No, need to apologize, I understand." Alberto answers.

The doctor says.

"As I explained earlier, your husband is in a very critical condition. He has suffered a massive heart attack. He is in intensive care and will be there for a while if he overcomes these three days. Everything depends on God."

When the doctor leaves, Lucia introduces her mother to Alberto. Alberto looks at Lucia's mother and tells her.

"I am sorry to meet you under these circumstances."

Gabriela doesn't respond, just gives him the bag and tells him.

"Here you have some food."

Alberto doesn't know what to do, he doesn't understand why Gabriela is treating him that way. Lucia tries to intervene to lower the tension.

"My mother brought you this dish. She knows you haven't eaten."

Alberto takes the bag. "Thank you very much. You shouldn't have bothered."

Gabriela does not respond. It is obvious she does not like Alberto. Alberto leaves so as not to get in the way.

"I will leave now. If you need me, don't hesitate to call me."

Gabriela does not thank for what Alberto did and only tells him.

"My daughter brought your vehicle. It is in the parking lot."

Lucia responds. "No, mother, I will take it."

Why do you have to take it if that is his vehicle?

"He doesn't know how to drive." Lucia replies.

"He has a car, but he doesn't know how to drive and now you want to take him. Well, I don't think so," Gabriela ironically replies.

"Don't worry ma'am, I take a taxi, anyway, Lucia will keep the pickup truck for now, she needs it and that way there will always be someone with Don Gregorio, otherwise you had to take Lucia home and come back again, they only allow one person to stay with him."

"So, you don't know how to drive?" Gabriela reiterates.

"No ma'am, I don't drive." Alberto responds, a little upset,

"Enough mother, I will take him as it is obvious. He bothers you too." Lucia replies.

"No Miss, you don't leave here with anybody. I will take him, and that's the end of it." Gabriela replies.

Alberto couldn't take it anymore; his patience reached its limit.

"No! No one takes me. I will take a taxi and here is your food. Thank you very. Much. You shouldn't have bothered."

Gabriela is surprised, but Lucia is happy.

"Well said, enough of putting up with injustices. It's time you put your pants on."

Gabriela is visibly angry. She tells her daughter to shut up and then tells Alberto.

"You don't worry about your three thousand dollars. I brought the checkbook to give you your money back."

Alberto looks at Lucia and tells her. "Maybe you can understand this, because I can't."

Lucia sadly tells him. "Forgive me Alberto, I don't understand why they have changed this way either."

"I don't care. That's their problem if they want to hate me. They won't get me to hate them, I will just ignore them. There is no place in my heart for hatred. I only ask God that you don't change. I will see you early on Monday. We must pay the engineers."

Alberto looks at Gabriela and tells her. "Have a good night and God save your husband."

Alberto turns around and leaves Gabriela with her hand outstretched with the check.

Gabriela tells her daughter.

"Jesus! He is so rude. You saw how he left me with my hand outstretched and did not take the check. Who that hell he thinks he is? We have two hundred thousand dollars in the bank. We do not need his miserable three thousand. I don't know how he is not ashamed to be here in the hospital all muddy with grease."

Lucia couldn't stand it anymore and said.

"When dad was between life and death, he did everything possible to keep him alert and came with me without caring about his appearance or caring that dad had slapped him three times. He paid the admission with his money without thinking twice and you resent giving him a plate of food knowing that he was hungry. Even knowing all his good actions, you humiliated him without even giving him the benefit of the doubt. I don't recognize you."

Lucia runs after Alberto, who was leaving in a hurry. She catches up to him and tells him.

"Forgive me, this is not fair."

Lucia hugs Alberto, who tells her. "For you, I take this and much more. I love you like I have loved no one in my life."

Lucia kisses Alberto, and the two of them kiss passionately.

Lucia tells him. "Promise me you will never change."

"Only if you promise me you will never change, either."

Lucia hugs and kisses him again. "This is our second deal. Only in this one I demand 100%. Let me take you home."

"No, you need to be with your mother and your father. They need you." Alberto answers.

Lucia turns around and runs to her mother. Gabriela looks at her, horrified. Her dress is stained with grease again.

"What have you done? Look at you. You have grease stained all over your brand new dress. What a shame. Is that the education we gave you? You don't respect your father or me to throw yourself into the arms of a stranger."

"Mother, I don't have Alberto's patience. I'm an adult, even though for you I will always be a little girl. I love Alberto and if that's a reason to hit me, then don't wait to get home and start right now."

Gabriela was speechless. She understood that they, with their intolerance and unjust attitude, had thrown Lucia into Alberto's arms.

"I don't recognize you, Lucia."

"You are right mother, we've become strangers. I don't recognize you either."

"Go home. I need to be alone with your father."

Lucia looked at her mother with sadness.

"I'm going home. I never thought you would send me away from your side when we should be more united than ever. Think about it and I hope you reconsider."

That night Lucia came home, took her brand-new white dress stained with grease, hugged it and cried over it. She later puts it in a box and hides it in her room inside of an old trunk.

On Sunday morning, Lucia shows up at the shipyard and finds Alberto painting the office.

"What are you doing? Did you forget we are in going to church today?"

Alberto looks at her in surprise. "Sorry, love, I thought you would be in the hospital with your father."

"No, when I promise something, I fulfill it. You have to change fast because we are late."

Alberto quickly puts away the paint and says.

"I will take a quick shower and we'll leave."

"No time for shower, just change and we leave."

"But Lucy, I don't want them to say you're with a person who doesn't bathe."

"If I don't care what my parents say about you, much less I care what other people say about you, either." Lucia replies.

Lucia decides not to go to the church she usually attends. She goes to a new church close by. It was a modern style church and not so crowded. The priest noticed them immediately when they entered.

Alberto asks. "Is this where you come with your parents?"

"No, it's the first time I've come. God is everywhere, and that's what is important, plus here are not my mother's old gossipy friends."

"How is your father doing?

"Please keep quiet. We are already late."

At the end of the Mass, everyone greets each other and the parishioners, who are almost all elderly, surround them and introduce themselves kindly. The priest joins the group and greets them.

"Welcome to the house of God, which is also your home too. It gives us great joy to have you among us."

Alberto responds. "It's our custom to attend church. It's the first time we've come here."

"And I hope it's not the last. A young marriage in our ranks rejuvenates us all." The priest responds.

"We are not married yet." Lucia responds.

"Where are your parents?" Ask the priest.

"My parents are in Italy. Her father is in very serious condition in the hospital and her mother is accompanying him." Alberto answers.

"We come to pray for my father's recovery and my mother's understanding."

The priest takes the hands of both and tells them.

"I will join your prayers. With faith in God, everything is possible."

A couple in the group says. "Today we celebrate our 50 years anniversary and we have prepared a lunch to celebrate with the brothers and sisters of the church. We would love for you to join us."

Lucia looks at Alberto, waiting for Alberto to say something, but Alberto kept quiet. Lucia says.

"Alberto, say something. They are talking to you."

Alberto responds. "Love, you decide. I do what you say."

The priest intervenes. "You will not regret it. Every year Edma and Gaspar celebrate with delicious cakes." Finally, Lucia and Alberto accept the invitation and spend a pleasant afternoon which makes them forget all their problems for a while.

Lucia returns to the hospital to relieve her mother, who instantly asks.

"Where were you? I have called you four times, and you didn't answer."

"I went to church," Lucia replies.

"You are a liar. I called Berta, and she told me you didn't go to Mass."

"Mother, I went, but we went to another church and met some wonderful people."

Gabriela takes her daughter by the arm and, as if Lucia was a little girl. She tells her.

"What do you mean we went? While your father is torn between life and death, you are having fun with that boy."

"Mother, we went to pray for dad's recovery and then we were invited to the 50th wedding anniversary of a wonderful couple. Everybody there prayed for dad's recovery."

Gabriela doesn't want to keep listening and interrupts her.

"Listen to me. I can't relieve you early tomorrow."

"Mother, I must be in the shipyard tomorrow; I have to pay the engineers."

"Well, they will have to wait because I have to go to the bank. We do not have checks. I wrote the last one for that idiot Alberto, who left me with the check in my hand. I must pay five thousand to the hospital on Monday. This is the best hospital, but also the most expensive. A week in intensive care costs five thousand dollars. Thank God we have enough money in the bank. We can afford that and much more. You don't need to work, let alone be with that idiot."

"Mother, let's not argue please, you need rest, please I need you here as soon as possible tomorrow." Lucia hugs her mother and enters to see her father.

Monday morning, Gabriela enters the bank and goes straight to see the manager.

"Good morning, Mr. Morgan. I need your help."

"Sure. How can I help you?"

"My husband is in intensive care at Francis Hospital, and I have to pay five thousand dollars today, but I don't have checks. I urgently need provisional checks to make payments."

The manager opens his eyes and says. "My God! Five thousand dollars, that's crazy."

Gabriela, in a gesture of haughtiness, responds. "That's nothing. We already paid three thousand dollars. Thank God that Gregorio has enough to cover the expenses in case his treatment requires staying in the hospital for three weeks."

The manager gets up from the desk and responds. "Please wait a moment while I'm going to print you some provisional checks."

Gabriela worries. Almost twenty minutes had passed, and the manager had not returned. When the manager returns, he only brings three checks in his hand. Gabriela annoys says.

"How are you going to give me just three checks? I need more."

The manager sits down, fixes his tie, puts his hands on the desk, then lowers his head and scratches his forehead. Gabriela notices the manager wants to say something, but he can't say it.

"Don't feel bad if the printer is not working. I come another day, but let it be known this is not professional and leaves much to be desired."

The manager looks at her and tells her. "The check for three thousand has not been cashed yet."

"Yes, I know that." So what? What's going on? Replies Gabriela, a little annoyed.

The manager raises his eyebrows and moves his head from side to side, but does not speak.

"Just talk once and for all. I don't have all day." Gabriela tells him.

"It is that when they cash the check of three thousand and then the check for five thousand, the account will be left with only six hundred dollars."

Gabriela felt a twinge in her heart that prevented her from breathing. She turned red and hardly could speak.

"You have made a mistake; we have two hundred thousand dollars in the account. Please check again."

"No, mam, that's why I took my time. Your husband made several transactions, but in the end, there were only ten thousand left and then he has spent one thousand four hundred."

Gabriela takes the checks and gets up, she could only think of Gregorio, she would have to take him out of the hospital and that would be fatal, she also wondered what had happened to the money and if there was a relationship between Gregorio's strange behavior and the lost money. Gabriela was pale, her sight clouded, and she collapsed to the ground. The manager and other employees ran to assist Gabriela, who looked in dreadful condition. The manager calls an ambulance and Gabriela is transported to the same hospital where Gregorio was admitted. The bank manager remembers Gabriela had mentioned Lucia was in the hospital taking care of Gregorio in the intensive care unit. He calls the hospital to inform Lucia that her mother is on her way in an ambulance. A nurse approaches Lucia and asks.

"Excuse me, young lady, are you Lucia?"

"Yes, I am."

"We were informed your mother fainted on the bank, and she is being transported in an ambulance to the emergency. It will be better for you to go there to be with her."

Lucia runs out to the emergency room while asking God not to be anything serious. Once in the emergency she learns that her mother has been admitted. Lucia, extremely overwhelmed, asks the nurse.

"What happened to my mother?"

"We only know that she lost consciousness, and the doctor is examining her. Just wait, the doctor will be with you soon."

Lucia understands she cannot go to work and calls the engineers to transfer the appointment for the next day in the afternoon. Then she calls Alberto and Alberto hears her crying and thinks Gregorio has gotten worse.

"What has happened, love? Your father has worsened?"

"No, my father is still the same. It is my mother who is in the emergency now."

"But what happened to her?"

"I don't know. I haven't been able to talk to her. I just want you to know I canceled the appointment with the engineers."

Alberto quickly says. "Thank you love, I'm going out to the hospital in a few minutes."

"Yes please, I need you. I am running out of strength." Lucia replies.

Alberto looks at Daniel and tells him.

"You will be alone again. Do not accept work, but you can deliver the finished ones. In the receipts is how much you must charge."

Dany looks at Alberto with a frightened face.

"Yes, but don't be late, please."

"I don't know if I will come back. If at 6:00 PM I haven't come back, you close the business and leave."

Alberto changes his clothes and takes a taxi straight to the hospital. Upon arriving at the emergency room, he finds Lucia talking to the doctor.

"Doctor, how is she?"

"Obviously, because of stress plus another emotional shock produced her collapse. She is sedated, and we keep her under observation. If she reacts well, we will discharge her this afternoon."

Lucia thanks the doctor and goes to the reception, the receptionist tells her.

"Your mother's bill is a hundred and twenty. And if you are going to pay it together with your father's bill, then it's five thousand one hundred and twenty."

"Yes, I will pay them together, but I must enter my mother's room to get the checkbook."

Lucia enters her mother's room and sees her mother is totally sedated. She searches her mother's wallet and takes out a check, then goes to the reception and makes the payment. Alberto and Lucia decide to wait in the emergency for Gabriela to wake up. Alberto and Lucia sit holding hands, waiting. Forty minutes later, the nurse comes over and says.

"Your mother is awake. You can come to see her now, but try not to get her excited or upset. She must rest."

Lucia enters the room and sees her mother lying with her eyes closed with tears streaming down her cheeks. Lucia understood her mother's pain was not a physical pain, that something very serious had happened and she did not know what it was. Lucia did not know what to do. If she inquired into what happened, she could worsen her mother's situation, but how can she help her if she did not know what was happening? Lucia sat next to her mother, gave her a kiss on the forehead, holding her hands, and said nothing. Her mother burst into tears and Lucia hugged her and whispered.

"I don't know what's going on, nor do I care. I just want you to know you are not alone, that together we will move forward."

Gabriela squeezed her daughter's hands and kissed them.

"Thank you, Lucy. You and your father are all I have and love in this world."

Lucia caressed her mother's hair for a long time without either of them uttering words. After a while, Gabriela takes a deep breath, draws strength and asks her daughter.

"How is your father?

"It's still the same. The doctor told me that at least it hasn't gotten worse, but his condition is still critical, that we should keep praying for a miracle."

Gabriela stares at her daughter and caresses her. Lucia has a bad feeling, but she can't guess what it is.

"Lucia, I must get out of here right now."

Lucia looks at her in amazement.

"No, mother, the doctor should discharge you. I don't want more scares. With dad is enough."

Gabriela sits on the bed and responds.

"No, Lucia, this hospital is very expensive; we can't afford it."

"What do you say that? Money doesn't matter. What matters is your health. I just paid for dad's week and your admission. It was only five thousand one hundred and twenty. The doctor says that dad may be two or three more weeks if all goes well."

"Do you think it's nothing's. That is a person's year salary?"

"I know it mother, but you are worth much more than that to me." Lucia replies.

"Daughter, is that we have no money, we can't afford it."

"What are you saying? You have access to dad's account and there is enough to cover it?"

"Which part do you not understand? There is no money."

Lucia was paralyzed. Her face changed completely.

"You can't be serious. Maybe dad was putting the money in a separate account, and you didn't ask the bank for that information."

"No Lucia, I don't know what happen, but your father has no money and now that you paid such an amount, we have only six hundred dollars left."

Lucia drew strength from deep inside, trying not to lose control. Now she understood why her mother had fainted. Lucia tightly clenched her mother's hands.

"You have always told me that God never abandons us, and it is time to have faith and not decay. We cannot move dad from here.

That would kill him. You make sure you recover as soon as possible. I will take care of the rest."

"What are we going to do, Lucy? Even if we mortgage the house, it is not enough to pay even a week and a half."

Lucia took control of the situation and told her mother.

"You get out of here as soon as possible and go straight to dad's room and wait for me there until I come back."

"But what are you going to do?"

"I'm going to solve this problem. Sitting here won't solve it, but dad will get out of here only when he is fully recovered."

Lucia goes straight to see Alberto, who sees her with tears in her eyes and hugs her.

"What happened to your mother?"

"My mother fainted when she found out that Dad had no money in the bank. We do not know what has happened, but there is no money. She knows that if we take him out of this hospital, it's a death sentence."

Alberto takes her hand and says. "You know what mine is also yours. Take money out of the account and pay it."

"We can't. The engineers demanded to put the payment in a separate escrow account to ensure payment. We cannot touch that account; it is in the hands of the lawyer."

Alberto responds. "We can ask for a loan against the business for thirty thousand. I am sure there will be no problem."

Lucia looks at Alberto in surprise and asks.

"Are you sure of what you are saying?"

"I can lose anything but my word. I can't believe you ask me something like that, but first we must go to see a lawyer."

"Why a lawyer?" Asks Lucia.

"Because you have to be an owner, only that way you can get a loan to solve this problem. I must remain working. Now more than ever, we have to produce."

Lucia hugged Alberto and cried. She could not believe what she heard. The man her father hated the most without a second thought was determined to save his life. They both went to see the lawyer to make the legal changes to include Lucia's name in the business. That gave her the power to sign without Alberto's signature.

Lucia shows up at the bank and looks for the manager. "Good morning, Mr. Morgan. I need a big favor from you."

"Good morning, Miss Lucia. I am at your service."

Lucia presents him with the documents that made her part owner of the business and asks for a loan of thirty thousand dollars. The manager takes the documents and looks at them and tells her.

"Lucia, I know that the situation with your father is urgent, but given the circumstances, by the way quite abnormal, the strange financial transactions of your father and the sudden appearance of your name in this business the bank will take much longer to verify all the documents."

"How long will it take?"

"Two weeks, maybe longer."

"I can't wait two weeks. I have to pay five thousand a week. That's the hospital cost."

The manager moves his head and responds.

"I'm sorry, but the bank is very strict. I don't want to get you excited, but if the loan application is in Alberto's name alone, I think the process will be much faster. The bank would look at it as an incentive to win Alberto's business account."

Lucia joins her hands in a plea.

"Please, Mr. Morgan, start the process on Alberto's name only. The business data is the same and he will come to sign this afternoon. I beg you. It is an emergency."

"I shouldn't do it. It is against the procedures, but I know it's an emergency and they will be prepared to sign this afternoon. We can approve the loan in four days, but if Alberto doesn't show up today before 5PM. You can forget about the loan."

Lucia stood up like a spring. "Thank you, Mr. Morgan. We will be back at four this afternoon."

Lucia drove to the business and informed Alberto of the situation. Alberto immediately looked at Dany and said.

"Be prepared that today you will close the business again and from tomorrow you will do the work of the office every time Lucia is out."

Dany opens his eyes. "But Sir, I have never filled out those papers."

"Do you know how to read and write English?" Alberto asks him.

"Yes, sir."

"Well, then you are ready to start today."

Alberto hugs Lucia and tells her. "Everything will be fine. Let's give him time to prepare the papers. In the meantime, go back to the hospital and bring lunch to your mother."

Lucia returns to the hospital and finds her mother had left the emergency room and was in Gregorio's room. Lucia asks her mother.

"Did the doctor let you go, or did you leave?"

"Lucy, I had nothing else to do there. I'm fine."

Lucia shakes her head; she knows that her mother will not listen, and that it doesn't worth arguing.

"Here you go, mom. I brought you lunch."

"Thank you, Lucy. I feel weak, this will help me. What did you accomplish?"

Lucia replies. "I'm working on that I don't want to talk about until I have something concrete."

"Can I help you with anything?" Ask Gabriela.

"Yes, pray for this to have a happy ending."

Lucia shows up at the shipyard to pick up Alberto who is working on an engine.

"Wait Luci, I will change right away."

"There is no time. You are good just like this. Let's go."

Lucia and Alberto enter the bank, and the manager greets them. Lucia comes forward and says.

"Mr. Morgan, here is Mr. Alberto. He comes to sign the loan documents."

The manager looks at him and sees Alberto stained with grease.

"Let me look for something for you seat on."

"Don't worry, we won't sit down. We won't stain your chairs." Lucia responds.

The manager looks at her and says.

"Thank you for your understanding. I talked to the main office and if you open an account in this bank as part of the loan agreement, you will have the loan approved in three days."

Alberto, right away, responds. "Consider it done. We will open a savings account right now."

After signing the documents, Alberto asks Lucia to return him to the shipyard, because he must finish the engine he is working on.

"No sir, eat first. We will go to a cafeteria and have lunch together. I bought lunch for my mother, but you must eat too." Lucia replies.

"Love, I am too dirty to go eat in a public place. It is better if we buy food on the way to the business, and we eat together there."

"Okay, if you'll feel better that way."

The next three days were very tense. Gregorio's life depended on the loan approval. Lucia had not revealed to her mother where the money would come from to pay for the hospital for fear that her mother would oppose. She went twice a day to the shipyard to supervise the work that had been delegated to Daniel and to bring food to both. Alberto worked 15 hours a day to keep up with the increasing demand, since he was creating a reputation for a fast and professional service.

On the day of the loan approval, Lucia shows up at the shipyard and sees Dany arguing with a client. Lucia calls him aside and asks him.

"What's wrong Dany?"

"It's that the man doesn't want to pay the taxes. He says we told him his job cost sixty dollars and he will just pay sixty."

Lucia looks at the young Daniel, who was visibly angry and tells him.

"You are in charge of this business. We accept your decision as the right one."

Lucia wanted to see if Dany could do a good job and correct him if necessary. Dany looks at Lucia, moves his head sideways and responds.

"Well, I'll figure it out my way and you fix it if it doesn't suit you."

"Perfect, so it will be." Lucia replies.

Dany takes the client's work receipt and asks him.

"How long have you lived in this country?"

The client looks at him and responds disparagingly.

"What the hell does that have to do with what we're talking about? Listen brat, I was born and raised here. You all are the foreigners."

"Perfect then taxes are nothing new to you." Dany replies.

"Yes asshole, but the taxes are not included in the receipt, so the total price is sixty, including taxes." The customer responds.

Dany takes the stamp and cradles the receipt and hands it to the customer.

"Here you go, Mr. Thomas. Your job is only sixty and you can take your boat. Just remember you have no guarantee and if something happens, take it somewhere else because we will not take care of it."

Dany's response made two customers laugh. The customer reddens and responds.

"You are wrong, boy. The guarantee is implicit in receipt."

"Mr. Thomas, the receipt says nothing about the warranty, but if you pay the taxes, we can add the warranty to you at no cost." Dany replies.

"Okay, I will pay the taxes, but you must include the guarantee in writing." Scream the customer.

"It will be as you say, Mr. Thomas."

The customer paid his taxes and left the premises under the mocking smiles of the other customers. Lucia rubs her hand over Dany's head and says.

"Well-done Dany, I wouldn't think it myself. I think you took my job."

Alberto enters the office, but this time he is well dressed. Alberto tells Dany.

"Take the orders from these gentlemen and go home early. You deserve a break, but tomorrow I want you here early."

"Thank you, sir. I promise you I will be here early."

Alberto and Lucia go to the bank, Lucia is very nervous, because if they deny the loan, she must take her father out of the hospital and take him to a clinic where the seriousness of her father could not be treated properly due the lack of resources. The manager sees them entering the bank and goes out to receive them.

"I have good news for you. Your loan is ready, and I could get a .05% interest rate reduction."

Lucia puts her hands up to the sky and says.

"Thank God, and you too, Mr. Morgan, finally a ray of light in this long, dark tunnel."

"It's a pleasure to help loyal customers. What is the relationship between you and Mr. Alberto?"

Lucia without a second thought answer.

"He is my future husband; we are just waiting for my father to get better to get married."

"I congratulate you. You make a beautiful couple." The manager responds.

After leaving the bank, Alberto and Lucia decide to go to an Italian restaurant to celebrate. For the first time, they are alone and without the pressure of the problems that do not stop raining on them. Lucia takes Alberto's hands and tells him.

"Promise me we will be together forever."

Alberto replies. "I just hope your father gets better, so we could get married, but you know he hates me."

"I hope he changes and understands our love is a true love, but if he does not accept you, that will be his problem. I am an adult, and no one can force me to marry or not to do it."

Lucia and Alberto leave the restaurant and go to the hospital. When they arrive, they see Gabriela, who runs towards Lucia and hugs her.

"What has happened, mother? Why are you crying?"

"It is out of happiness. Your father has opened his eyes and I think he has recognized me. The doctor says his condition is still critical, but this is a positive sign."

Gabriela completely ignored Alberto. She kept talking as if Alberto was not present. Lucia suddenly tells her.

"Mother, we have more good news, but you must eat first. You are very pale."

"Tell me, Lucy, don't make me wait."

"No, you must eat first, and then we talk. Alberto brought you food."

Gabriela looks at Alberto and gives a non-sincere thank you. Hearing Alberto's name diminished the joy on her face.

"Thank you. You didn't have to bother. I have no appetite."

Alberto is tired of so many reproaches. He answers her.

"Mam, the only sin I have committed is to love your daughter with all my heart. I love her and respect her. I want you to know I will never hate you, even though you do not accept me. For me, hatred does not exist, and you are the parents of the person I love. That is enough reason for me to love and respect you, even if it is not reciprocated."

Lucia says. "Mom, please do not damage the moment and eat that. We have brought it for you with all affection and if you do not eat, there is no news."

Gabriela reluctantly responds. "Okay, I'm going to eat it, but believe me when I say I don't have an appetite."

Gabriela ate, trying to pretend that she was not hungry, but in the end the smell and good taste of the food overcame her.

"It was delicious, thank you very much. I really needed it, but now please tell me the good news."

"We've solved the money problem; we don't have to take dad out of the hospital."

Gabriela jumped for joy and hugged her daughter, crying out of joy.

"How did you do it, Lucy?"

"Mr. Morgan gave us a loan at the bank." Lucia replies.

"But, how come? We have nothing to collateral, a loan, and it takes a lot of money to pay your dad's bill?"

"Mom, Alberto and I applied for the loan using the business as a collateral and they approved it."

"You mean Alberto, because you have nothing to do with that business."

Alberto intervenes and responds.

"You are not wrong, she as my future wife owns 50% of everything and her name is already registered as an owner."

"Future wife! Who has given you permission?"

Lucia responds. "God has given us permission. I hope you and my father have no objection."

Gabriela did not know what to answer. She felt anger, but the mere fact of saving Gregorio's life contained her, and she felt some gratitude.

"What do you say, mom? Aren't you happy?"

"Yes, Lucy, I will be eternally grateful to both of you, but I want you to marry out of love and never out of pressure."

"Then you have nothing to worry about and a lot to celebrate." Answers Alberto.

Gabriela understood it would be like swimming against the current and that it was not the right time to fight. She took Alberto's hand and asked him.

"Do you love your mother?"

Alberto looks at her in surprise.

"What kind of question is that? "My mother is sacred to me."

Gabriela, still holding Alberto's hands, answers.

"I just want you to know that every woman is sacred to someone, so they all deserve the same respect."

CHAPTER SIX

THE WEDDING

A month had passed since Gregorio's departure from the hospital. His recovery astonished everyone, given that all the prognoses had been against him. The news that his daughter would marry Alberto was a stone in Gregorio's shoe, but he cleverly decided not to oppose it and to be on the lookout to destroy the wedding before it took place.

Gregorio and his wife were looking for something to use against their future son-in-law, but they could find nothing. Thanks to Alberto and their daughter, they could save Gregorio's life, and the business had prospered. The space previously occupied by John O'Connor's business became a warehouse for yacht engine parts and marine supply, monopolizing the local market. Above the warehouse, there was a cafeteria restaurant, which was always full of customers and workers from around the area.

Lucia and Alberto's friendship with their new church friends, Edna and Gaspar, had solidified. The priest, known to all as Father Geronimo, holds a mass to bless the two new businesses of Lucia and Alberto. Through father Geronimo, they met Luz, a Peruvian emigrant who specialized in seviche and seafood dishes. He also introduced them to a Russian emigrant named Viera, who was a specialist in Slavic and French cuisine. Gabriela supervises the cafeteria, and she added the Italian flavor to the menu.

Gabriela and Gregorio have not accepted their daughter's marriage. They had only changed tactics and joined the business, trying to find something that could unmask Alberto. Lucia and Alberto had set a date for their wedding. They should finish the accumulated work to take a week off for the honeymoon. Lucia's parents seemed to agree with the wedding because they knew their daughter would marry with their blessing or not.

Gregorio and Gabriela are sitting on the bed, looking at each other without saying a word. Gregorio breaks the silence and asks her.

"What have you been able to find?"

Gabriela shakes her head, somewhat depressed.

"Nothing. The cafeteria works like a normal business. We are only three people. Luz, Viera, and I. We are so busy that we can't cope. We will have to hire at least two more people. I am aware of everything, and nothing strange has happened."

Gregorio shakes his head and says.

"I oversee the warehouse. I have checked all the boxes coming and going out, but I have nothing either. I asked Lucia to hire someone for the warehouse under the pretext that I should not lift heavy loads. When they hire my assistant, then I can go around the docks to check."

One morning, Gregorio finishes up with a client. When Tony enters with his two bodyguards, Dino and Caino. Gregorio felt his blood pressure rise to the maximum just by seeing Tony. Tony approaches the counter and tells him.

"Good morning, Don Gregorio. What a way to prosper. I thought you would retire as you had told me, but your business has become famous in town."

Gregorio takes a deep breath; he tries to control himself to avoid ending up in the hospital again.

"You are wrong. None of this is mine and you know it. I have only stayed a while longer because I need a job thanks to you stealing my business and my savings."

Tony just looks at him and smiles.

"You are wrong. Thanks to me, you have become famous. Everyone talks about Don Gregorio's shipyard. You should charge him for using your name. That neon sign you put up can be seen from all over the river. All the captains know your name. You are quite a celebrity; I should be your agent."

Gregorio held back, took a deep breath, and slowly felt his blood pressure return to normal. Gregorio pulls out his notebook and replied.

"I will take your order. What do you need?"

"I need a new anchor for my yacht, but since I found you here, now I have in mind something else. We will talk about it another time; I must first make some contacts and then I will contact you."

"You are wrong. None of this is mine and you know it. I don't give a damn about what you have in mind." Gregorio answered emphatically.

Gregorio goes to the back of the warehouse and returns a few minutes later with an anchor, puts it on the counter and says to Tony.

"Here you have your thing. If you need nothing else, have a good day."

Tony looks at him and smiles, then looks at one of his bodyguards and says.

"Dino, I think Don Gregorio needs to have his memory refreshed."

Dino, helped by his great size and long arms, grabs Gregorio behind the neck with his left hand and pulls him towards him, almost raising him on the counter. Dino put a revolver under Gregorio's jaw and says.

"Ungrateful, if you are free, it is only because of Don Tony. Do not think it cannot change. Don Tony could contact the authorities and tell them that his conscience does not allow him to sleep knowing the crime you committed."

Alberto opens the front door of the warehouse and recognizes Tony. Tony greets him.

"Hello Alberto, nice to see you."

Tony touches Dino on the back and says to Dino.

"Dino, enough hugging Don Gregorio. I did not know you were so close to him."

Dino hides his revolver in the holster that he carries on the side and pretends to have been hugging Gregorio. Dino knew they could not touch Alberto or relate him to any mafia activity.

"Don Gregorio reminds me so much of my uncle that I can't help it. Forgive Don Gregorio if I over did it."

Tony congratulates Alberto for his success in the business.

"When Marcelo contacted me to find you a shipyard, he told me it was your family tradition. But when I saw you so young, I never thought you had so much talent in this field.

Alberto shakes Tony's hand and gives him a hug.

"You don't know how much I appreciate everything you did for me when I arrived. I will always be in debt to you."

"Don't need to mention it. We Italians help each other selflessly. Isn't that right, Don Gregorio?" Tony asks.

Alberto notices that Gregorio's face says quite the opposite and thinks there has been a problem with Tony's request.

"Is everything all right with your order? Alberto asks.

"Yes, totally satisfied, you have it all. You will see my face more often from today on." Tony replies, then gives Alberto a big hug and leaves.

Gregorio had just convinced himself Alberto was not only a mobster, but that he was Tony's boss. Only that could explain Tony's reaction.

Alberto asks Gregorio. "Did anything happen to Tony or any of his bodyguards?"

Gregorio looks at him seriously and responds.

"What would you do if I said yes?"

Alberto looks at him seriously. He would allow no one to bother his future father-in-law. But that same firmness of gaze reaffirmed Gregorio that Alberto was a mobster of a much higher rank than Tony.

"I will allow no one to come to our business to cause trouble and if Tony is a problem, you let me know. To me, people who walk around with bodyguards do not inspire confidence. I was planning to invite him to the wedding, but I changed my mind."

Gregorio does not know what to answer. He turns his back on Alberto and leaves, saying.

"It's your wedding. You choose your guests."

That night Gregorio says to his wife, Gabriela.

"Today I have been able to verify that Alberto is with the mafia, but he is not of low rank. He is of a higher rank than those who walk with bodyguards. Today a well-known mobster came to the business and when he saw Alberto, he almost kisses his hand. Unfortunately, it is not the material evidence we need, but we are heading in the right direction."

Gregorio and Gabriela were still looking for Alberto's hidden business, but they found nothing. They had exactly one month left to stop the wedding. But they had only the assumptions that Alberto was a bandit, against the facts that Alberto worked from morning to night and that, thanks to him, they were paying Gregorio's medical bills.

One night, Gregorio is driving home alone in his vehicle when a police patrol unit turns the overhead lights on him and orders him to stop his vehicle. Gregorio stops by the side of the road. He did not understand what had happened since he was not speeding or had committed any infraction. Gregorio is concerned to see a civilian car stopping in front of him and then back up, blocking him. Gregorio sees a police officer getting out of the police car and lights his face with his flashlight, blinding him momentarily.

"Good evening, Gregorio. I stopped you to greet you and to refresh your memory." The uniformed man says.

The uniformed man turns off his flashlight and Gregorio could see there two silhouettes instead of one, but the light blinded him and could not distinguish the faces. Gregorio rubs his eyes, trying to recover his vision, and distinguishes who were those silhouettes next to his vehicle. They were Tony and Lieutenant Clark, the same one who, along with Tony, had blackmailed him when they forced him to sell his shipyard. Tony puts his hand on Gregorio's shoulder through the window and says.

"It took us time to find you alone, but here we are. We will contact you to give you the exact information of what you must do. We just need to make a few more contacts and then we start."

Gregorio, enraged, answers.

"Do not count on me. Neither you nor your boss, Alberto, is going to include me or make me smuggle anything. You can tell that to Alberto. Better yet, I'll tell him that myself tomorrow."

Tony opens the car door and pulls Gregorio out, holds him by the collar of his jacket.

"I will not be happy if you go with this gossip to Alberto. Just consider yourself a dead man if you do that. He knows nothing about us, nor should he know. If Alberto finds out about us, you will spoil my business and I will not forgive you."

Lieutenant Clark takes out his gun and puts it to Gregorio's head.

"As you can see, I kill you right here and nobody will find out, but that's very easy. I prefer to put you in jail for homicide so that you regret it every day of not having collaborated with us.".

Tony says. "I am finished for today. I'll contact you when everything is ready."

Tony then says to the lieutenant. "Make sure he understands that this is not a game, that he must do everything we tell him to do."

Tony leaves, and Lieutenant Clark tells him.

"Tonight, you will sleep in jail, turn around and put your hands behind your back."

Gregorio can't believe what's going on, but before he can say anything, the lieutenant handcuffs him and pushes him inside the vehicle. The lieutenant gets inside the patrol car and says.

"I stopped you for speeding, then you started arguing with me and pushed me. That's a crime, so you'll be in jail tonight. I will drop the charges, if you give an apology in front of my superiors tomorrow. If you don't, you'll be there until a judge hand down a sentence. But remember, you're going to do what we'll ask you to do, anyway. Tonight, it is only so you understand we are not playing, nor are we intimidated by you."

That night, Gregorio spent it in jail. All night long, he was thinking about why Tony didn't want Alberto to find out. He concludes Tony was doing some kind of business without Alberto's approval. That was the only logical way to explain what had happened. Gregorio thought to ask Alberto for help, but he changed his mind. That would get him deeper into the mafia. His biggest concern was his wife and daughter. He had never spent a night out of his house.

At 7 AM, Lieutenant Clark shows up at Gregorio's cell and says.

"I talked to my captain. I told him not to present any charge against you if you apologize in front of him. It will be as if it never happened. If you refuse to do so, you will spend about two months in jail before you get out. Either you work for us or return to prison, but the next time for the rest of your life."

Gregorio needed to be free to fight the mafia, so he had to give in once again to Clark and Tony's injustices and blackmail. Gregorio was taken from his cell to the captain's office, where Lieutenant Clark was also waiting. The officer who transferred Gregory was leaving when Lieutenant Clark orders him to remove Gregorio's handcuffs. The officer looks at him, confused, and asks.

"Are you sure of that, lieutenant?"

"Yes, I am sure. The prisoner has calmed down and deep down, he is not a troublemaker. He only needs to control his temperament."

The captain says to Gregorio.

"You are lucky. The lieutenant has insisted on not bringing charges against you. I want to clarify that your actions are totally unacceptable. Explain to me what leads you to commit such stupidity."

Gregorio takes a deep breath; he understands that to fight Tony and Alberto; he needs to be free. To achieve that, it will mean accepting the guilt of something he did not do. Gregorio tries to control himself. His anger and helplessness are so great, he fears he will lose control and slap Lieutenant Clark right in front of the captain.

"I do not know what happened to me, sir. I had a terrible day at work and perhaps I did not realize I was driving over the speed limit."

The lieutenant interrupts.

"You remind me of my uncle. He was a very hardworking and noble man, but of a very explosive temperament. That brought him many problems. I arrested you for two reasons and they are not because you were driving at a high speed. It was for arguing with me and then pushing me. I did it to give you the help I couldn't give my uncle. Maybe if someone had done to him what I did to you, he would have changed. You are a hardworking and honest man. After this experience, you will appreciate your freedom and your family a little more. I'm sure you don't want to repeat mistakes that could land you in jail again."

Gregorio did not answer. He clearly understood that it was a warning from Clark. He continued with his gaze down and couldn't hold back his tears of humiliation and helplessness. The captain stands, shakes hands with Lieutenant Clark and with a gesture of admiration says,

"I congratulate you. There are few uniformed men who take the time to educate the citizens. Our job is not just to punish and to enforce the laws. It is also our duty to understand that citizens are people who sometimes make mistakes and deserve a second chance. Your actions help us gain the trust and respect of the citizens, which is our final goal."

The captain's words gave Gregorio a glimmer of hope. He thought that perhaps all was not lost, but he had to be careful because he did not know if the captain was part of the mafia. Gregorio raised his head, looked the captain in the eyes, and thanked him. The captain replied firmly.

"It is not me you should thank, but the lieutenant, and I would like to hear it."

Gregorio used his rage to draw strength to respond. He thought he would thank Lieutenant Clark for making him understand war was inevitable and that he would fight to the end without fear.

"Thank you very much lieutenant, you have made me understand that in life one has to change a lot. That sometimes we don't do the right thing and that in the long run it has consequences."

Gregorio thought to himself that if he had done the right thing and had not accepted the first Tony's favor, this would not be happening to him now. Gregorio turns to the captain and says.

"Captain Steve, your words have made me see the light at the end of the tunnel. Today, I am a new man with faith in a system which I often distrust."

The captain sees sincerity in Gregorio's face, comes up to him, shakes his hand, and then says.

"We are all here to protect and serve. You pay our salary. There will always be a rotten apple in the sack, but that does not mean that you should not eat apples or that you have to throw the sack away."

Lieutenant Clark tells him. "Your car is not in the city yard, as it should be. It is parked in front of the station. You can take it whenever you want."

Clark gives him the keys to the car and says.

"Do not take my actions as a punishment. They are an investment in society. I hope your regret is sincere and we will all benefit from it."

Gregorio goes straight to the business, where he found a police car parked in front. He wondered what was going on. He will end it all once and for all. When he is a few steps from opening the door, Alberto comes out with the officer and sees him. Alberto, visibly worried and upset, asks him,

"Where have you been? Your wife and daughter are heartbroken, and you haven't even called them. You may not care for me, but you should care about your family and your family cares about you. It's not fair what you've done to them."

Alberto says to the officer.

"Forget everything, officer, and thank you for coming, but Mr. Gregorio, as you can see, is not missing."

Alberto's attitude made Gregorio understand Alberto knew nothing about what happened, but for him, that did not remove Alberto from the mobsters' list. Alberto, in another tone, says to Gregorio.

"Forgive me, Gregorio, if I spoke to you that way. It was not my intention. I was worried about you. I have looked for you in all the hospitals. I drove the road to your house several times to see if he could find your car."

Alberto puts both hands on his shoulders and whispers.

"I even went into those striper's clubs to see if I could find you."

Gregorio reacts by giving him a push and yells at him.

"How dare you think about me like that? Maybe you are used to visiting those places or maybe you own one, but I've never in my life set foot in one of those places."

Alberto replies: "I apologize, but understand that you made me do it and you are also to blame for not telling us."

Gregorio saw sincerity in Alberto's eyes and, a little calmer, he answered.

"If you want to know what happened, come inside and I will tell you. But if you want to know the details, ask your friend, Lieutenant Clark."

"Who are you talking about? I don't know any Lieutenant Clark. This is the first time I've spoken to a police officer, and it was to report you missing."

Gregorio did not answer him and entered the office. He saw his daughter and wife sitting, hugging, and crying. The two got up and ran to hug him.

"Where the hell were you?" His wife yelled at him.

"I spend the night in jail." Gregorio responds coldly, waiting for Alberto's reaction.

Lucia and her mother are frightened, and Alberto joins the group.

"In jail! What happened?" Shouts Lucia.

Gregorio responds angrily.

"Nothing that your boyfriend doesn't know. A certain Lieutenant Clark stopped me and accused me of driving at high speed and then arrested me, saying that I had pushed him, then dropped the charges in the morning after humiliating myself in front of the captain. I had to apologize for something I never did to avoid going to jail for three months."

Alberto could not contain himself and responded.

"You accused me of all your problems. The customers who come here are the only ones I know of. I have spent the entire night looking for you throughout the city, and that is the way you thank me. I have done nothing to you other than to help you, and I have helped you more than you deserve. That will be your problem if you want to be ungrateful."

Alberto left, visibly upset. It was the first time Alberto had responded to Gregorio in that way. Gregorio understood Alberto did not know Lieutenant Clark, but that did not remove him from his list. Lucia stared at him and said.

"Father, I do not recognize you. My mother and I are witnesses. You are alive, thanks to Alberto. He has been unconditional to our family, and now you accuse him of what happens to you. You have slapped him unfairly in front of me. Explain once and for all what is the problem you have with him."

Gregorio did not answer, and Lucia left in search of Alberto. Gabriela and Gregorio are alone in the office. Gabriela tells him.

"I think you overdid it with Alberto. I witness he was looking for you all night."

Gregorio shakes his head and answers.

"Maybe you are right, but tonight I will explain everything to you and then you will understand me better."

Alberto and Lucia's wedding was a week away. Vittorio, Alberto's father, arrives from Italy for his son's wedding. Alberto gives him his room in the shipyard and prepares a small room in the warehouse for himself. Vittorio works in the warehouse with Gregorio, so he won't get bored. One day, when Vittorio and Gregorio were alone in the warehouse, Gregorio was totally frustrated that he could not stop the wedding. He decided to vent his frustration with Vittorio.

"Don Vittorio, I want to be honest with you. I have never approved of the relationship between our children. I know I owe my life to your son, but I owe all my misfortunes to him as well."

Vittorio was surprised. Now he understands why Gregorio had treated him coldly. Vittorio was sitting in front of Gregorio, both staring at each other without saying a word. Vittorio breaks the silence and says.

"It will be good for you to say everything that bothers you. Leave nothing inside. I also wouldn't want my son to enter a relationship that could fail."

Gregorio moves his head and answers.

"You are right. I do not plan to hold anything. I also do not want my daughter to enter a relationship and then divorce when she discovers she has been deceived. I admit my daughter adores your son, and maybe your son also loves my daughter, but the values in which I have educated my daughter do not agree with the values of your son. In our family, there is no place for bandits."

Vittorio flushes, takes a deep breath. He is a little short of slapping Gregorio, but he holds back and slowly replies calmly but firmly.

"Now you will have to explain yourself, and I hope you have evidence to support your offense."

Gregorio felt relief inside. He will have the pleasure of unmasking Alberto in front of his father.

"Very well. I hope you have the courage to listen until the end. As a parent, I understand that sometimes children deviate from the training they receive at home. If this is the case, I am very sorry and add to your pain. I am the victim of blackmail from a mobster, who forced me to sell him my business. That mobster not only forced me to sell him my business, but he stole all my savings by fooling me during the purchase. That mobster later appears with your son and says that your son is the new owner. I'm not sure if your son is the boss of that mobster, or if they have separate businesses. Not only did they steal my business of so many years, now they want to force me to smuggle for them or they will put me in jail or charge me of a terrible murder that I did not do."

Vittorio moves his head tormented; he looks worried. Gregorio believes Vittorio is unaware of the fact that his son is a bandit. Vittorio asks.

"Have you seen, uncovered, or heard of any criminal activity in which Alberto was involved?"

Gregorio worriedly responds.

"That is the problem. I have no way to prove it, but that mobster brought him here as a king. Two days ago, that mobster was blackmailing me right here. Even one of his thugs had the barrel of his revolver under my cheek. When they saw Alberto enter, they hid the gun and little lack to kiss his hand. I told them I would talk to Alberto about the matter, and they threatened me. They told me I couldn't say anything to Alberto. Everything shows Alberto is above them."

Vittorio had both of his hands on his forehead and moved his head from side to side. Gregorio thought he was right, that Alberto was a bandit, and that his father didn't know. Gregorio felt sorry for Vittorio and says.

"I'm sorry, but you better find out now. Maybe you can steer him in the right direction."

Vittorio punches the table and shouts. "Damn you!"

Gregorio gets up, intending to leave, and says.

"Now you can understand that this is a failed marriage before the start."

Vittorio answers: "You are totally wrong, and now it is your turn to listen."

Gregorio stops, looks at Vittorio, and sees that Vittorio is furious. Gregorio sits down to listen to Vittorio. He thought he would hear an apology from Vittorio, and he says.

"What can you tell me I don't know? Better tell me what we are going to do."

Vittorio replies. "On the contrary, you know nothing, and it's better you find out now."

Gregorio is shocked. What else could it be? Perhaps father and son are also gangsters.

Vittorio takes a deep breath and says.

"I too was blackmailed by the mafia. They forced me to sell my shipyard. That was our family's legacy for three generations. The difference is that the bandits who blackmailed me were people of word and honor. They promised to get a shipyard in America for my son and assured me that the mafia would never bother my son. What is the name of that bandit who blackmails you?"

"His name is Tony." Gregorio replies.

Vittorio picks up the phone, beckons Gregorio to come over, and says.

"We're going to sort this out right now."

Gregorio looks at him, a little confused, but approaches to listen. Vittorio calls Marcelo, who oversaw getting into the shipyard for Alberto in America.

"Hello Marcelo, this is me Vittorio."

"Hello Vittorio, I'm glad to hear from you. Where are you calling from?"

"I have come to my son's wedding." Vittorio replies.

"Congratulations, you should be thrilled."

"Yes, but I really want to ask a few questions."

"Ask whatever you want." Marcelo responds.

"Who is that Tony who brought my son here?"

"He is an acquaintance who owes me several favors. What happened? Is there a problem?" Marcelo asks with interest.

"Did you warn him he couldn't touch Alberto?"

"Yes, he knows it and also knows that it comes from far above. I assure you he would not dare to do such stupidity. But you worry me. What's going on? He knows he can't touch Alberto." Marcelo answers in the affirmative.

"It is that he has been blackmailing Alberto's future father-in-law, even forcing him to sell his business and, in the process, stealing two hundred thousand dollars, practically the work of a lifetime."

Marcelo takes some time analyzing the situation and asks him.

"Did he meet that person before or after he met your son?"

Vittorio gives the phone to Gregorio, who at first hesitated to take it, but then he takes it with anger and answers.

"Don Marcelo is me Gregorio, Alberto's future father-in-law. I met Tony before he brought Alberto. He put a bomb in the business next to mine where four people died and then blackmails me using a police lieutenant who is another bandit, telling me they will charge me with that crime if I don't do what they want."

Marcelo takes his time and then replies.

"Don Gregorio, we function totally different. There are rules that whoever does not comply with them pays dearly, so I assure you that Tony will not mess with Alberto, but if he had dealt with you before meeting Alberto, that exonerates him unless he messes with Alberto. This Tony is not of my confidence and is a guy of medium rank. If you want, I will take care of him."

"No thanks, it is unnecessary. You have already helped me enough with clarifying the situation. You have a good day."

Gregorio hangs up the phone and stares at Vittorio. Vittorio asks him.

"Why did you hang up on him? That man owes me his life. I got him out of the Island of Ischia when they were looking for him to kill him. If we ask him for help, he will help us."

"I don't want help from the mobsters. For accepting Tony's help, I'm in this mess. I don't want to owe anyone anything. You helped him knowing he was a bandit. That is why bandits do not disappear, but multiply."

Vittorio responds. "I helped him not because he was a bandit, but because he was an ex-partisan who fought with me during the German occupation. He also risked his life for me, and to me, that is totally different."

Gregorio changes his attitude and answers.

"I lived through that time, and I have admiration and respect for what you did, but he is still a bandit. I do not want his help."

"So now what?" Question Vittorio.

Gregorio shakes hands with Vittorio and says.

"The first thing I will do is congratulate you for having a son like Alberto. I have been wronged all this time, and I have been unfair to him, I have humiliated him, provoked him even to the point of hitting him hoping that he will hit me back, but his love for my daughter is greater than anything I have done to him. I want to give him a big hug and apologize for how unfair I've been to him. Then I will prepare for war. I will not allow these bandits to fuck me. If I will die, it will be fighting."

Vittorio, while holding Gregorio's hand, responds.

"You are not alone. If they want war, they will have it. Remember that we are a family. What affects you, affects your daughter, what affects your daughter affects my son, so it involves me as well. We are going to teach these bandits that you don't play with the old guys. Vittorio and Gregorio give each other a big hug and say at the same time. "For our children."

The friendship with priest Miguel and the members of the church grew stronger. Edna and Gaspar took the task of organizing Alberto y Lucia's wedding. Edna and Gaspar had no children and referred to Lucia and Alberto as their adopted children. Gabriela's friends refused to attend Lucia's wedding if the wedding wasn't held it in their church. Gabriela tries to convince her daughter to transfer the wedding to the church where they had always attended.

Gabriela takes her daughter's hand and says.

"Lucia, I don't think it's right you celebrate your wedding in a church you just met. We have attended our church since before you were born. My friends see it as a betrayal to our priest. I also feel uncomfortable. Your father agrees with me on this matter. You can invite Edna and Gaspar to our church. We will welcome them."

Lucia gently, but firmly, replies.

"Mother, in the most difficult moments of my life, when even you were against us and dad was between life and death, your friends, instead of helping me, criticized me. They even spoke badly of Alberto without knowing him. The only thing they showed was their hypocritical friendship. These people opened their doors to us when we needed it the most. They offered their help to us selflessly. Your friends are putting their vanity and pride above their supposed friendship. If they decide to come, they will be welcome and if they decide not to come, they will not be missed."

All the members of Alberto and Lucia's church were present at the wedding. Gabriela's friends did not attend the wedding, and that bothered Gabriela a lot. The members of the church decorated the church for the wedding as a gift for the new couple. It surprised Gregorio and Gabriela to see the great fraternity that existed in that parish. They made them feel as if they were all old friends. Gregorio couldn't help the tears, and broke protocol when he walked his daughter to the altar. He hugged and kissed Alberto on the cheek. It was a moving ceremony for everyone. As they exited the Church, the bells ran, and everyone applauded and threw rice at the new spouses.

Gaspar and Edna, along with the members of the church, had prepared a reception for them at their homes. Alberto and Lucia could not afford the honeymoon, the money was not enough. The expenses of expanding the business and payments to the hospital kept them counting the pennies. Alberto refused his father's help. His plan was to continue living in the business with his wife for as long as it was necessary.

Gaspar and the photographer were waiting for them in a brand-new Cadillac to take them to a surprise reception. He made them believe he would take them to the shipyard. Gaspar tells them.

"My tenants moved out and I must stop to check on that house for a moment, if you don't mind."

Lucia answers. "Of course, Don Gaspar."

They stop in front of a small but beautiful house. Gaspar exits the vehicle and pretends to struggle to open the door. He comes back to the vehicle and asks Alberto.

"Alberto, can you help me open the door, please? I am having problems with this key."

Alberto gets out of the vehicle, and Gaspar asks Lucia.

"Lucia, come with us. It is going to be just a moment. I want your opinion about which color I must paint the living room wall."

Lucia gets out and the three of them walk to the house. Alberto takes the keys to the door, puts it in, and turns it.

"I don't understand why you have problems; it turns very easy."

When Alberto opens the door, the house is darked, and they heard a group of people screaming:

"Surprise!"

Lucia sees her mother and hugs her.

"Mother, did you know about this?"

"Yes, Lucy Gaspar told me. This was his idea. I could not spoil the surprise."

Gabriela hands her a bag Lucia had given her in the morning and tells her.

"Lucy, here you have the bag with clothes you gave me this morning."

Lucia goes into a room and changes her clothes. She puts on the same white dress stained with grease she wore the evening her father had a heart attack. That evening, she decided she would marry Alberto and be with him for the rest of her life. When Gabriela sees her daughter wearing the dress, she cries and hugs her.

"You cannot imagine how much I regret what I told the two of you that evening. How happy I am I was totally wrong."

The party continued late into the night. The young Daniel surprised everyone with his musical talent. He played the guitar and sang Italian folklore sons. When all the guests leave, Gaspar and Edna approach Alberto and Lucia, give them the keys to the house, and say.

"This is the house in which you are going to spend your honey mon. This is the first house we bought, and it means a lot to us. We know you will take good care of it."

Alberto returns the key and says. "We thank you infinitely for your kindness, but we cannot accept it. Our business produces a lot, but the debts we have are also quite a lot. We have invested everything we have and owe a heavy debt to the hospital. We can't pay the rent for this house, and we wouldn't accept it for free either."

Edna laughs and responds.

"Who said it would be free? We will rent it for seventy dollars a month. I know you will take care of it as if it was yours."

Alberto, lowering his head, answers. "We would love to, but we cannot afford it. Lucia and I are not getting a salary and it will be like that for another two years. Our debts have priority. It is our word and our credit."

Gaspar puts his hand on Alberto's shoulder and responds. "Your father told me you refused his help."

"Yes, he has already done enough for me. I would feel useless if I can't do it on my own." Alberto answers.

Gaspar moves his head and tells him.

"You are a businessperson and a man of your word. I like that. I propose a deal."

Alberto, surprised, asks him. "What deal?"

"I rented this house for seventy a month, but the tenants moved to Texas after living in it for twenty-one years. They were like family to us, and we want you to take care of it as the previous tenants took care of it. You will start paying in two years. You will pay one hundred and fifty for two years. After that, you pay eighty-five a month."

Alberto doesn't answer, but Lucia says. "Yes, we accept."

Edna hugs her and says. "You did the right thing, Lucy. Men are afraid of everything, plus I am terrified that other people rent the house and destroy it."

CHAPTER SEVEN

ALBERTO BECOMES THE LEADER

Gregorio and Vittorio forced Alberto and Lucia to take a week off for their honeymoon. Vittorio was in charge of the mechanic shop, Gregorio oversaw the warehouse, Daniel the accounting, and Gabriela managed the cafeteria. Everything was going well until the day Tony entered the warehouse.

Vittorio sees Tony arrive and, at that moment, he realizes Tony was a mobster because of his bodyguards and his way of dressing, but not like the mobsters he met in Italy. This was a thief and a low-class bandit. Tony tells Vittorio in an imperative way.

"Hey! Go look for Gregorio. I need to talk to him."

Vittorio, undeterred, responds.

"I'm sorry, sir. Gregorio is not here at this moment. Can I help you?"

Tony looks at him from top to bottom and replies.

"My business is with the circus owner, not the clown."

Vittorio approaches the counter and points his finger at him.

"That's a big mistake. The clown is the soul of the circus. There is no circus without a clown."

Tony looks at him seriously and replies.

"What's wrong, old man? Are you tired of living? "If you are in a hurry to go to the other side, I can help you."

Vittorio smiles at him, shakes his head, responds.

"I'm not afraid of that trip, nor am I clinging to stay. We're all passing through. The time I have left here, I prefer it with emotions before I do boredom."

Dino, Tony's bodyguard, took it as disrespect and tried to grab Vittorio through the counter, but Tony got in the way. "Leave it Dino."

Dino stops and points his finger at Vittorio.

"Don't play with fire, because you are going to get burned, you stupid old man."

Vittorio had managed to get Tony's attention, which was his goal.

"That I am an old man is true. On the stupid part, you are wrong and finally I am not afraid of fire. In the end, I know I will go straight to hell."

Tony laughs. "You know, old man, at first, I didn't like you, but I can see you have balls. I think you and I speak the same language."

Vittorio puts both hands on the counter, leans forward, and responds firmly.

"Then talk, and I'll tell you if we understand each other."

Tony stands in front of Vittorio and answers.

"I need one of the empty boxes with the business logo on it."

Vittorio stares at him and replies.

"If you're going to use our boxes, be sure to use a medium size so you don't raise suspicions. The shipment must leave from here, therefore, before the merchandise goes out, we must receive an order. Finally, you better deal with the clown, because I don't think that the owner of the circus has the balls to do something like that. When you work with fear, things never work out."

Tony was impressed. He had never heard that answer before. He extends his hand to Vittorio, giving him a firm handshake, and he says.

"Not only do we speak the same language, but we also think the same. What is your name?"

"My name is Vittorio, and I had to leave Italy when things got a little hot. An old friend got me this place to shelter me until things cool down and I can come back."

Tony instantly tied up the dots and asks.

'Is your friend's name Marcelo?'

Vittorio puts on a surprised face to reaffirm Tony's suspicion.

"I'm sorry, but I don't divulge information unless it's necessary."

Tony pats Vittorio on the shoulder and says.

"You are from the old guard. Surely the one who brought you here put a condition on you that you cannot violate."

Vittorio laughed and pointed at Tony asks.

"Were you banned too?

"Yes, and you don't have to tell me who brought here. I know who it was."

Vittorio responds. "For the record, you said it. I said nothing."

Tony asks him in a low voice.

"What's the mystery with that boy?"

Vittorio shrugs and responds.

"I don't know. The only thing I can tell you is that he is a stupid young man who is protected from the top, so if you treasure your balls, stay away from him. He gave me a room in the shipyard, so I live here. As you will see, Gregorio is not any good for you. He lives outside of here. Your merchandise may leave during the day, but it must enter at night."

Tony slaps on the counter and screams.

"Beautiful! You were sent from heaven. I was about to kick Gregorio's ass."

Vittorio puts his hand on Tony's shoulder and says.

"If Gregorio is in this, then I am out. Don't count on me. That asshole is going to sink you, and I want no more trouble. But remember that my 15% is non-negotiable."

Tony is happy. He believes everything is taken care of. He firmly tells Vittorio.

"Vittorio, don't damage the moment 10% and there is no negotiation on that."

Vittorio squeezed Tony's hand. "Ok, we have a deal."

Vittorio leaves and returns with three empty boxes with the company logo and tells him.

"Choose which will be the best, so I will buy them to avoid suspicion."

Tony selects the medium box, and Vittorio tells him.

"Take it with you and when you know how many you need, give me a phone call at night."

Tony puts a twenty-dollar bill in Vittorio's pocket.

"You earned it. This is your first payment."

Half an hour later, Gregorio arrives at the warehouse and Vittorio tells him what happened. Gregorio is frightened. He walks around in a circle scratching his head.

"I knew he was coming back. What are we going to do now?"

Vittorio, shrugging his shoulders, responds.

"I don't know, but at least he won't bother you anymore. We will think about that when we find out what they want to do."

Lucia and Alberto had returned to work. The business prospered and was very popular among the locals, but the many debts from the hospital, the expansion of the business, and the loan interest, kept them at a minimum wage. One night, Tony contacts Vittorio and tells him.

"Today, around 2:AM, a boat with merchandise will arrive. I need you to take care of it. Caino will then give you the addresses where you will send the boxes with the names and the amount that each box must carry."

"Who is Caino?" Question Vittorio.

"He's one of my men."

"If the boxes must carry a certain weight, send me a scale with Caino. I have nothing to weigh here." Vittorio replies.

"Don't worry, I'll send it to you with Caino."

That night, Vittorio received Tony's merchandise, which was twenty kilos of marijuana.

Vittorio kept the drug in a corner covered with a tarp and lay down to sleep. In the morning Gregorio wakes up Vittorio, who was exhausted from having worked almost all night.

"What's wrong Vittorio? You look like you did not sleep last night?"

"It's because I didn't and now, we have to decide what to do." Vittorio responds with a bewildered face.

Gregorio understood that the moment had come. A paralyzing cold ran all over his body, his eyes widened, and tears ran down his chicks without being able to avoid it. Gregorio tried to speak, but he couldn't find the words, nor did they come out of his mouth.

"My God, what a misfortune. Damn those bandits." That was the only thing Gregorio could say, and he sat with his elbows on his knees, covering his face. Vittorio approached him and put his hand on his shoulder and tried to comfort him.

"You are not alone, and we must confront this problem head-on without hesitation. They're going to regret meeting you."

Gregorio did not respond. He remained in the same position, only moving his head from side to side as bewilderment. Vittorio calls out his son to inform him of the situation. Gregorio felt someone approaching and tried to compose himself, wiped his tears and stopped.

"What do you want, father? I hope it's fast. I'm with some customers?"

Gregorio keeps his back to Alberto; he knows his face will give him away. He was sure that if Alberto sees him in that condition, he will realize that something is happening.

Vittorio tells Alberto.

"Come over son. I have to show you something."

"Father, you can show me that later. I told you I am busy with some very important clients."

"Son, it will only be a moment and then you leave if that is more important."

Alberto turned his eyes upwards and answers.

"Come on dad, show me what is so important, but hurry, please."

Vittorio walks to the corner where the drug was hidden, gives a pull to the canvas that covered it, and says.

"This is what I want to show you."

Gregorio, terrified, turns and sees the twenty kilos of marijuana packed in the corner.

Alberto innocently asks.

"What is that? Where did it come from? Did you buy it? You know we are short of money. We only buy what is necessary and Lucy must approve it. She is in charge of purchase."

Gregorio felt sorry for Alberto and a great guilt. He had always accused Alberto of being a mobster and now he sees Alberto is a naive young man and that because of him, not only Alberto, but the whole family is in danger.

"That's drugs son, it's twenty kilos of marijuana."

Alberto paled and looked at Gregorio's face. He sees Gregorio is as frightened and pale as he is. Alberto thinks Gregorio is unaware of what is happening and deduces that his father is the author of the contraband. Alberto stands in front of his father, and with fire in his eyes, tells him.

"You should know that if I don't slap you right now, it's out of respect for you being my father, but I won't let you put my family's peace in danger. We are hardworking and good people. Shame on you, this is totally contrary to the values of our family. Return that drug immediately and if you can't return it, throw it into the sea. You also have 24 hours to pick up your things and return to Italy."

Gregorio is moved to see Alberto's attitude. He is proud of him; he feels a great relief to know that his daughter has a husband with all the qualities that he had sounded.

Gregorio intervened and standing in front of Alberto tells him.

"You are wrong son; your father is not to blame for this. It is I who is to blame for everything."

Gregorio does not finish speaking when Alberto raises his hand and slaps him, throwing him to the ground. Alberto's fury is indescribable. Gregorio didn't think Alberto was that fast and didn't even see him raise his hand. Gregorio is sitting on the floor, totally stunned. He feels a ringing in his left ear as if it was a disconnected phone and moves his head circularly, as if he is about to fall.

"You are a dirty old man, you scoundrel, you son of a bitch! How dare you do such a thing! That's why you didn't want me to marry Lucia, so you could keep smuggling. You are a bastard portraying yourself as a saint and selling drugs. You remove that drug from here and you disappear from here, too. Don't dare to set foot in this business again, I don't want to see your face ever."

Vittorio takes his son by the shoulders and shakes him tightly.

"No, son, is not what you think. Gregorio has never sold drugs."

Alberto, instead of calming down, becomes more enraged and points to Gregorio, who was still sitting on the ground as the one who was coming to himself.

"So, when the business was his, he never sold drugs and now he's going to use the business to sell drugs. He doesn't mind fucking his daughter for the sake of fucking me."

Vittorio, in an authoritarian voice, shouts.

"Neither one. Sit back and listen to what's going on so you can understand what happened here. You shouldn't jump to conclusions before you know everything."

Alberto is out of control, in a sudden movement pushing his father's hands off his shoulders.

"Sorry father, there are no circumstances that can justify that drug in my business, or you also think that I am stupid."

Vittorio angrily yells at him.

"I said sit down and listen or you too are going to get a slap. This is a family problem that we have to solve together."

Alberto defiantly responds to his father.

"There are no drug traffickers in my family and if you have drug traffickers in your family, that will be a family that I don't know or want to know."

Vittorio knows his son fast. If he tried to slap him, Alberto would block him, so he does as if he is going to slap him, and when Alberto tries to block him, he kicks him in the genitals. Alberto is taken totally by surprise. He fell to his knees, his eyes turned back, and he is about to faint. Vittorio hugs him and says fondly.

"Sorry son, you must find out things you did not know, and they will not be very pleasant."

Curiously, Alberto is kneeling next to Gregorio and Vittorio is in front of them as if he is telling a story to both of them.

Vittorio tells him.

"Listen to me to the end. You will understand things are not the way you think they are. I will begin by telling you that when I refused to sell Don Franco our shipyard in Italy, I was kidnapped by Don Franco's men and brought before him. Don Franco told me that orders came from above. I had to choose between the shipyard or my son."

Alberto, still in pain, replies.

"Father, you always told me Don Franco was your friend, that he was a man of honor, and now I come out with that he was a mafioso."

Vittorio sits on the floor, and the three of them sit on the floor like three children who are playing.

"It is true, Don Franco is my friend and thanks to him not only saved your life, but we sold our shipyard for three times its cost. They promised to buy a shipyard in America for you and that they would never bother you. Don Franco contacted Don Marcelo to get you a shipyard. Marcelo delegates that to a certain Tony who is a thief without honor."

Alberto interrupts him.

"Father, since when have there been any gangsters with honor? They are criminals who do not respect life, much less the law."

Vittorio tells him with character.

"Don't interrupt me, stupid. Or do you want another kick?"

Gregorio had already recovered and could not hold back the laughter from Vittorio's comments. Alberto, angrily, turns to Gregorio.

"What the fuck are your old the fox laughing at? I already lost all respect for you."

Vittorio slaps Alberto's head.

"Shut up and don't interrupt me. Tony, before being contacted by Marcelo, already had plans to blackmail Gregorio by accusing him of the murder of three people who Tony himself had murdered. Tony not only forced Gregorio to sell him his shipyard but stole all his savings. That's why Gregorio hated you so much. He thought you were part of Tony's gang."

Alberto addresses Gregorio in anger.

"Why did you never tell me anything, you asshole? Why didn't you call the police?"

Gregorio responds calmly.

"I can see that you don't know those people. What's more, they protect you, and you didn't even know it. Your father understands the seriousness of the situation. Tony has the police on his side. Lieutenant Clark works for him. Do you remember the night I spent in jail? Lieutenant Clark stopped me when I left and for no reason took me to jail. He told me this was the beginning, that if I did not cooperate in the smuggling, I would go to jail for the three homicides and I would never see my family again."

Alberto moves his head from side to side and says.

"I understand now why you didn't call the police. But, why didn't you tell me anything?"

"I didn't want to worry you, son. You had already saved my life once; you already did a lot for me." Gregorio replies in sorrow.

Alberto takes a deep breath and stays thoughtful for a moment, then says.

"Well, I'm already aware. I must go to see the client who is waiting for me. We will talk later."

Vittorio sees Alberto is going to get up and stops him.

"No, son, that's not all. Mine is still missing."

Alberto, more than sitting, collapses to the floor.

"! Oh Good!, this can be true. What did you do now?"

Vittorio, with a terrified face, tells him.

"Tony came looking for Gregorio and I attended him because Gregorio was out. I was aware of the situation and since I knew Don Franco and Don Marcelo, then I posed as a mobster who had to run away and was hiding here. I told him that Don Franco had sent me here until things calmed down for a bit. I acted like a mobster and gained his trust. Now he wanted to deal with me instead of Gregorio. He distrusts Gregorio, but he trusts me."

Alberto did not come out of his amazement. He listened with his mouth open as if he was a zombie. When his father finished, Alberto asks him.

"What is your plan? What will we do now?"

Vittorio shrugs his shoulders and opens his hands and responds like a scolded child.

"I don't know, I do not know. I've worked all my life honestly. I'm not a criminal."

Alberto stands with his hands on his head.

"My God, what the fuck have you two done? Father, you fought in the resistance against the Nazis, along with Don Franco and all those mobsters."

"Yes, son, but we were young and fighting against a foreign invader. This is totally different; these are unscrupulous criminals." Vittorio replies.

Alberto sees that Vittorio and Gregorio are still sitting on the floor and tells them with character.

"Get up. We have to work; we will talk about this before we go home tonight."

Vittorio and Gregorio ask Alberto.

"That was it? There's nothing more to say?"

"You are right. This is a family problem, and everyone should know it. I hide nothing from my wife. If you had done the same, maybe things would have been different. The family is all of us, not just us three."

Alberto leaves angrily, slamming the door so hard that almost knocked it down. Gregorio and Vittorio looked at each other. Neither of them had seen Alberto so angry and showing so much leadership.

At the end of the day, Alberto gathered his wife and mother-in-law in the warehouse and showed them the drugs. Alberto told them everything that had happened before. Gabriela and Lucia cried inconsolably. Now Lucia could understand her father's attitude toward Alberto.

Gabriela had in her hands the bread she was carrying for breakfast the next day, but when she heard the story, she throws it on Gregorio's head while screaming at him.

"How could you keep quiet about something like that? Is it that we are not trustworthy to you? We have been with you through thick and thin, and you told your problem to Vittorio before us."

Alberto intervened and brought order to the meeting, taking absolute control of the situation.

"This is not the time to argue the past. The problem is in the present and from now on, no one can keep a secret. We are all in this together and we all will emerge victorious in the end together."

Vittorio, worried, questions.

"How, son? We are not criminals, and we cannot go to the police."

Alberto stares at his father and answers.

"You always told me you trust me, so everything will go well. I also remember that you told me that the time would come when I would be the one who would have to take the reins of the family, that you would step aside and that you would trust me just as Grandpa did with you. Well, that moment is now, and you will have to trust me. We will all take part in this fight together, but there can only be one captain."

Vittorio is proud of his son. The women were calmer. Only Gregorio doubted Alberto's maturity and said.

"I don't think you have the experience that is needed to face these criminals."

Alberto stands in front of Gregorio and replies.

"If I were you, I would keep quiet, because if someone has not shown knowledge of how to fight them is you. You are the one who lets yourself get into this problem and you do not know how to get out of it. To that, I must add my dad's experience who thought the way to fix the problem was to join them, fill in the warehouse with drugs, and now tells me he does not know what to do."

Lucia and Gabriela stood next to Alberto and both staring at Gregorio and Vittorio, told them sarcastically.

"You guys already helped a lot with getting us into this problem. It's better for Alberto to take the reins from now on."

Gregorio and Vittorio were quiet, sitting side by side like two punished kids. After what they were told by the women, they didn't say a word all night.

Lucia asks Alberto. "What's your plan?"

Alberto shakes his head and convincingly responds to her.

"Tony thinks I'm protected by the mafia and I'm not aware of anything, so that will stay that way. Tony is afraid of the mob bosses and knows that if he tries to get me involved in something, he will have to pay the consequences, so he will be very careful. Dad will continue to pose as a mobster. Gregorio will continue his role as a coward, who will do everything he is ordered. Gabriela will be our eyes from the second floor and as soon as they enter the parking lot, you will let us know."

Lucia asks. "What do I do? Or I am not part of the family?"

Alberto calms her with affection and responds.

"Simple love, yours comes according to what we need to do. The most important thing here is immediate communication between everyone, no matter how insignificant it may be. Every decision I make is an order, and no one can challenge or ignore it. Only then we can emerge victorious."

Alberto showed the firmness of a character that was hidden behind his kind face. Alberto became the leader of the family in which everyone put their hopes to get out of a great problem.

CHAPTER EIGHT

Vittorio Asks Marcelo for Help

Everyone had been waiting for Tony to show up in the warehouse, but three weeks passed, and Tony didn't show up. Since Tony had never given information on how to contact him, the situation was becoming more and more tense. The mere fact of having the drug stored in the warehouse made them all guilty of drug dealing.

One early Monday morning, Gregorio was having breakfast in the cafeteria when he saw Tony's car entering the parking lot. Gregorio immediately shows the car to Gabriela, then informs Alberto, Lucia, and Vittorio.

Tony enters the warehouse with his bodyguard Dino and Caino and is greeted by Vittorio, who follows Alberto's plan to the teeth.

"Good morning, Don Vittorio. Nice to see you again."

"Good morning, Don Tony. I think we have to clarify some points." Vittorio responds seriously, inspiring respect even though inside he was trembling with fear.

"What happened Vitto? What is the reason for that bad temper?"

Vittorio signals Tony to follow him. Dino and Caino follow him, but Vittorio stops them abruptly.

"Who told you that you could enter?"

Tony replies. "Calm down, Vitto, I trust them."

"Just because you trust them doesn't mean I should trust them. Trust is earned. It is not imposed or delegated."

Vittorio's response was so blunt that Tony turned around and told his men to wait outside. Alberto's plan was to create distrust between Tony and his men so that they would destroy each other.

Tony, angrily, complains to Vittorio.

"I am totally confident with my men, I understand you do not know them and that is the reason I told them to wait outside, but that disrespect to them damages my respect relation with them, so I hope this does not happen again."

Vittorio puts his hand on Tony's shoulder and says calmly.

"Tony, I'm much older than you. I can't be your father, but I could be your older brother. According to you, when this business takes off, you can be totally independent. That means the money will flow much more than before. Money is harmful to loyalty and in my years of experience, I can tell you I did not like the look of one of them."

"From whom?" Tony responds curiously.

"The chubby one, he rushed more than the other. It's like he wants to know too much. I have no problem with you seeing where the merchandise is, but he doesn't have to be sticking his nose where he hasn't been called."

Unknowingly, Vittorio had hit it right in the center. Even though Caino was not a traitor, his great curiosity had already caused annoyance for Tony. Vittorio saw that Tony's face changed, so he threw more gas at the fire.

"Don't get me wrong, and I don't want you to get rid of him. It's just caution. Please remember I am here sent by the bosses to hide for a while. If they find out I got in trouble here, this can end terrible for me. I also have the problem that I can't mix Alberto with anything. He is the protégé of Don Franco, Don Cristino and Don Marcelo. I still don't understand why, because in reality, that young man is an asshole and all he knows how to do is fix boat engines."

Tony laughs and replies. "We are in the same boat. Don Marcelo warned me strongly that I could not touch the young man because the consequences would be very severe. Protected child bravo! We risk our skin every day, so I had to buy him a business and be his driver as if he was my boss."

Vittorio smiles and responds. "I am in the same situation as you are, so our business must prosper to become independent."

Tony moves his head affirmatively and responds. "It's a shame I didn't know you before. You're like me. You can smell the blood from far away and know when to attack."

Vittorio lifts the tarp and shows him the drug hidden in a corner of the warehouse. "This can't stay here that long. You cannot leave a merchandise and disappear without leaving me a contact to communicate with you. What will happen if I must move the merchandize in case of an emergency? Remember that Gregorio and I are alone, and the less we deal with Gregorio, the better. Gregorio would not betray us because he knows it would also be his skin, but he is very clumsy and gets very nervous about everything."

Tony remains thoughtful and replies.

"You are right. I will give you a phone number where you can contact me or leave me a message. But I actually came here to tell you next week I will bring the list of customers for you to send the boxes to, as well as the amount of drug that each box should carry."

"Very well. It is necessary to move this drug out of here as soon as possible. It is that the little prince likes to walk around here from time to time, so we must do everything at night when he is not here."

Vittorio and Tony returned to the front of the warehouse, reuniting with Dino and Caino. Vittorio seizes the opportunity when Caino is behind Dino and Tony, so they can't see that Caino wasn't even looking at Vittorio.

"What the fuck is wrong with you? You don't scare me, asshole, if you have something to say, say it now and in front of everyone."

Tony and Dino turn around and see that Caino is nervous. Caino did not expect that, and it worked totally against him. Tony sees Caino is scared. He then looks at Vittorio and sees that Vittorio is annoyed and defiant. Tony falls into Vittorio's trap. He stood in front of Caino and said.

"If this old man tells you to jump, you just ask him how high. If he tells you to sit down, you lie down and if you have something to say, you say it now."

Caino paled. He understood Vittorio was plotting something, but he was afraid his boss would not believe him, and things would be worse for him, so he shut up and only apologized.

That afternoon, before leaving, they all met to discuss what happened with Tony that morning. Gregorio asks.

"What are we going to do now? Are these people going to force us to distribute that drug?"

Alberto thinks and responds. "That won't happen."

"But how? We have no alternative." Vittorio replies.

Alberto smiles and responds.

"You told me you had saved Marcelo's life. Now it's time for him to save yours."

"I don't want to deal with gangsters that will bring us more problems in the end." Vittorio responds angrily.

Scared, Lucia intervenes.

"Your father is right; we will become more entangled, and the goal is to get out of this as soon as possible."

"That's the way it will be, my love, I promise you." Alberto responds by giving her a comforting caress.

Alberto turns to his father and Gregorio.

"Listen carefully to the plan and do not deviate, so we will not have any surprises. In three days, you will call Tony and tell him that there is an emergency and that he must come to see you. You will tell him that for two nights in a row you have seen a car sneaking around the warehouse and that when you came out to investigate, the car fled. I will deal with Tony and Dino later. You and Gregorio will have an argument where Caino does not see you, but he can hear you. The goal is for Caino to tell Tony to create suspicions about my father. Tony will contact Marcelo to find out about you before distributing the drug. Marcelo will confirm the story that you are a mobster and that Don Franco protected you."

Vittorio and Gregorio look at each other without understanding.

"What good will all this do?" Gregorio asks.

Alberto puts his hand on Gregorio's shoulder, trying to get him to understand.

"This will make Tony blindly trust my dad and distrust Caino even more. I assure you that with one more push, Tony will eliminate Caino, and then we will make him believe Caino was not the traitor, but his chief bodyguard Dino."

Lucia, as a plea, tells her husband.

"Love, I think it's better that we sell everything and go away. We can pay off all our debts and have money left to start far from here. I could not live if any of you go to prison or is killed by one of those mobsters."

Vittorio and Gregorio join Lucia's request.

Alberto firmly replies to them.

"No, I will not run away from anyone. Father, you taught me that a man does not cower and must fight injustices. Wasn't it you who fought against the Germans during the Nazi occupation?"

Alberto then looks at Gregorio and asks him.

"Where is the brave man who slapped me and challenged me to fight? I need that guy here right now."

Everyone understood Alberto would not change his mind, that a long and dangerous struggle awaited ahead of them.

The next day, Vittorio left to visit Marcelo as Alberto had ordered. Vittorio went to the Little Nápole's restaurant, owned by Marcelo. Vittorio did not know how he would be received by Marcelo, because the last time he saw Marcelo, despite having saved Marcelo's life, Vittorio had despised him and called him a criminal.

Vittorio enters the restaurant, sits at a table, and when he is going to be served, he tells waiter.

"I need to talk to Don Marcelo."

The server knows he cannot take anyone to see his boss without prior authorization, so he responds.

"I'm sorry, sir, but Don Marcelo is not here, and he does not come here very often. If you want to leave a message, I will convey it to him as soon as possible."

Vittorio looks at him and shakes his head in the affirmative answers.

"Very well, tell him that Vittorio, the friend of Don Franco and Don Cristino, awaits him here and that he will not move from here until he sees him."

The server was used to calling the security who hit first and asked questions later, but this time he asked security to inform Marcelo of what was happening. Marcelo is in his office making a purchase of stolen liquor when he is interrupted by security. The security officer, named Galletano, is thirty years old, medium height, stocky and with an explosive temper.

Galletano enters the office and says.

"Don Marcelo, we have a situation outside in the dining room."

Marcelo raises his head slowly and responds sarcastically.

"Since when do I have to do your job? What do I pay you for?"

Vittorio had followed the server with his eyes and saw when he contacted Galletano. Vittorio gets up from the table and follows Galletano, but another restaurant employee stops him in front of the office by before entering Marcelo's office. The employee struggles with Victorio while screaming for security. Marcelo and Galletano hear the screams in front of the office, take out their pistol and go out to see what is happening. Marcelo sees that the server and a restaurant worker have a man pin down to the ground. Galletano starts to kick Vittorio while shouting.

"Your appointment will be with a doctor, not with Don Marcelo."

Vittorio was face down while being beaten by Galletano, so Marcelo didn't know who he was. The server tells Marcelo mockingly while enjoying the scene of the beating.

"I hope he learns his lesson. I told him you were not here, but the stupid man told me he would not leave until you see him. He says that his name is Vittorio and that he comes from a certain Don Franco and a certain Don Cristino."

When Marcelo heard those three names, he screamed and pounced on Galletano.

"Stop, animal, you are going to kill him."

Galletano stopped instantly, Marcelo had never intervened when they gave their due to an intruder.

"Are you sure Don Marcelo? I think this idiot has not received enough."

Marcelo pushes him and tells him.

"If you touch him again, I'll be the one who's going to kick the shit out of you."

Galletano and the server looked at each other. It was visible that they were more than scared. They had hit the wrong person. Galletano and the server lift Vittorio up from the floor and dust off his clothes, while apologizing to him.

"Excuse us, sir, we are so sorry. We didn't know who you were."

Vittorio, still stunned, extends his hand to Marcelo who, instead of shaking his hand, gives him a big hug. When Galletano and the server saw Marcelo hugging Vittorio, they both paled and disappeared like two dogs with the tail between their legs.

"What a welcome you have given me. Next time, I better send you a letter."

"Sorry Vitto, but neither they nor I knew who you were. What brings you around here?" Marcelo responds.

Vittorio, sadly, tells Marcelo. "I know I mistreat you the last time we met, and I apologize to you."

"Forget it, Vitto. You saved my life that night. I am the one who is indebted to you."

Marcelo sends for Galletano and the server who had beaten Vittorio. Marcelo goes to the server who was terrified and sweated as if he were in a sauna. "You are going to serve us dinner and make sure that it is exquisite because your life depends on it."

Marcelo then heads to Galletano. "Follow us."

Galletano felt butterflies in his belly. He was convinced that for sure he was not returning home and that if he was lucky, he would end up in the hospital. Marcelo takes Vittorio to a private room in his restaurant, where only very few people could enter, and orders Galletano. "You will stay outside and don't let even the Pope in. Then you will take Vittorio to the best hotel and stay watching over him until I tell you. You will do everything he asks of you and God saves you if I hear a complaint about you."

"It will be as you say, Don Marcelo, and do not worry, I answer with my life for the safety of Don Vittorio."

After chatting for a while and remembering the old times, Vittorio asks Marcelo. What can you tell me about that Tony, the one you commissioned to buy the shipyard for my son Alberto?

Marcelo did not expect that question. He understood that something was happening, and he was not aware.

As I told you before, he is a mid-ranking stupid jerk in the organization. He believes he should be in a higher position. He has had several brushes with the hierarchy, but he has known how to cover his shit by blaming others. I warned him he couldn't involve your son in anything, and I doubt he did because he knows he can't cross that line."

Vittorio responds. "He hasn't crossed that line and Alberto is not aware of anything that's happening."

Marcelo asks Vittorio. "What's going on Vito?" If you come here, it's because you need help. I must know everything so I can help you."

Vittorio tells everything to Marcelo, which he listens to without interrupting until the end. Marcelo raised a glass and said. "Let's toast"

"Why?" Question Vittorio in confusion.

"Because of your son's marriage and because you came to see me, that is worth a lot to me."

Marcelo lies back in his chair and stares at Vittorio and says.

"Listen to me without interrupting me just as I listened to you. Try to understand what I am saying because our codes of conduct are not common. In our organization, there are people with more honor and loyalty to their word than many politicians and ecclesiastical hierarchs. Everything that happened between Gregorio and Tony before your son Alberto appeared is totally legal before our codes. As long as Tony doesn't involve your son in any criminal activity, he has done nothing wrong. That Tony scammed Gregorio for two hundred thousand dollars and charges me too is not illegal either. That is unethical. He should not have charged me those two hundred thousand dollars and he should have given me half that is a hundred thousand because it was I who introduced him to that business. My duty would be to alert him you want to fuck him up, but I think the time has come for that stupid jerk to get what he deserves. You can count on me and my silence. I just ask you not to harm anyone else outside Tony's group and keep me abreast of everything. We do not approve of the sale of drugs because in the end we will end up destroying our own children, but that fight is becoming more and more difficult. That's a very lucrative business and if we don't do it, someone will end up doing it."

Vittorio was surprised by Marcelo's attitude. It was difficult for him to understand how a criminal attitude was perfectly legal for Marcelo, and even more so with the pride that spoke of his organization as honorable people. After dinner and the meeting was over, Galletano took Vittorio to the best hotel and was with him until the next day, when he took him to the bus station and made sure that Vittorio had left safely.

CHAPTER NINE

DEATH OF CANINO

On Monday morning, Tony, Dino and Caino show up at the warehouse. Alberto was immediately informed, and his plan was put in place immediately. Alberto and Lucia enter the warehouse and Lucia greets Tony and tells him. "Don Tony, let me introduce you to my husband."

Tony responds kindly. "I actually knew him before you, but I didn't know you got married. Congratulations."

"Thank you very much, Don Tony. My father and I will always be grateful to you. You gave us work when we needed it the most and when those thieves vandalized your yacht in our business, you understood and did not blame my father."

Alberto intervenes. "I had a wonderful impression of him, and Don Marcelo gave me a very good recommendation of him, too. We want to invite you to have breakfast in our cafeteria."

Tony did not want to raise suspicions, so he accepted, and Alberto pretended he had not noticed that Caino was with them and took Tony and Dino to the cafeteria. Tony said nothing about Caino so that he could finish as quickly as possible and go back to the warehouse.

When Tony and Dino went to the cafeteria, Gregorio asks Caino. "Aren't you going to have breakfast with the others?"

Vittorio mockingly responds. "No, he did not invite him. He knows that this fat man will bankrupt him if he invites him."

The goal had been met. Tony and Dino were separated, and Caino was alone with them and totally angry at Vittorio. Gregorio tells Caino. "Come with me to let me show you."

Vittorio does not let Gregorio finish the sentence. "That fat man may not enter the warehouse."

Caino flushed, clenched his fists, and closed his eyes, trying to restrain himself. Caino, in a calm voice, responds to Gregorio. "No, I'd rather wait until Tony comes back."

Vittorio and Gregorio stand behind a shelf high enough that Caino wouldn't see them, and close enough for him to hear them.

"You're playing with fire and you're going to get burned. You think Tony is stupid? Tony will discover that you don't know any Don Marcelo and that you're just a starving asshole. You got into his business and you're charging him a percentage like if you're a high-ranking mobster."

Gregorio and Vittorio tried to contain the laughter so as not to spoil the plan, because they could see through a crack the face of Caino's happiness.

Caino thinks that the time for his revenge has come. Caino is sure that this information is all he needed to prove to his boss that he is correct in his suspicions.

Vittorio takes his last thrust. "You don't have to worry; I just want him to give me his list of where to send the drug. I will take the drug personally, collect the money, and then disappear."

Tony and Dino return to the warehouse, and Vittorio tells Tony. "That cafeteria is fantastic. I've gained like ten pounds, but we need to talk about business before someone else interrupts us. Did you bring me the list to ship the merchandise?"

Tony pulls an envelope out of the pocket from inside his sack and Caino literally takes it out of his hand and tells Tony. "No sir, that's not the list. It is in the car."

Caino leaves for the parking lot and Tony and Dino are surprised, Vittorio and Gregorio look at Tony as if they are surprised too. Vittorio acts very upset and tells Tony. "Can you explain to me what the fuck is wrong with that fat man? I told you that there is something that I dislike about him. That is the reason that I have never let him even approach the merchandise."

Tony is furious, turns around and says nothing and goes out to find Caino. Caino is in the parking lot and when he sees Tony, he wastes no time and tells him.

"It's a trap. That brazen old man wants to take the information, deliver the merchandise, collect it, and disappear with the money. He doesn't even know Marcelo. It's all a story. You can't fall into that trap; you would be everybody's wiping boy and you would lose respect in the organization."

Caino has created a doubt in Tony, who does not know what to do but suspends the sale until he is sure that he is not in danger. Tony enters the warehouse and tells Vittorio. "We made a mistake on the list; we'll be delivering next week."

Vittorio punches the counter and says. "Fat traitor, I told you I didn't like him, that there is something weird about him. Leave me the list."

Tony replies. "I don't have it. That was the wrong list."

Vittorio stands in front of Tony and tells him. "If you want to play the role of an asshole, you can do it, but don't include me in that game. Now that fat man has the list and knows the contacts. I told you there was a suspicious vehicle loitering around here at night. Are you not convinced yet that something is wrong? If you do not deliver that merchandise, you will lose the trust of your buyers. There is nothing worse in this business than not delivering on time."

Tony remains thoughtful, but knows that the risk of being deceived by Vittorio outweighs the delay in the sale or losing a customer. "You're absolutely right, but we'll have to wait until next week."

That night they celebrated the first victory, they stop the drug sale and had created doubt about Caino in Tony.

"What's next son? Gregorio asks.

"What follows is clear. Tony will go to see Marcelo to confirm what Caino told him, but Marcelo will convince him that Caino has betrayed him. Tony even gave a bottle of wine to dad and took a picture with him, but his goal is to show it to Marcelo to be one hundred percent sure that they are talking about the right person. While Tony is visiting Marcelo, we will throw the drugs into the sea and make a police report of the theft in the warehouse."

Gregorio exclaims. "Are you going crazy? How are we going to tell the police that the drugs were stolen?"

Alberto laughs and responds. "No, we will throw the drugs into the sea and report a theft of two boat engines. Our goal is to involve Lieutenant Clark in this process. We must follow Caino and see who he meets so we can use the description of one of his friends' vehicles as the suspect's vehicle. Now let's toast courtesy of Don Tony."

Alberto took the bottle of wine that Tony had given to his father when he took the picture with him, and they toasted.

The next day, Tony shows up at Marcelo's restaurant and heads to Galletano. "Hello Galletano, I need to talk to Don Marcelo."

Galletano responds without paying attention to him. "You'll have to wait a while because he just walked into his private room. He's having dinner with a city councilman."

Tony stays thoughtful and then asks. "Do you have any idea how long it can take?"

"I do not know, but they just went in and that will be at least three hours."

Tony moves his head. "In that case, I will come to greet him and so he will know that I am here waiting for him."

Tony steps forward, and Galletano puts his hand on his chest, stopping him.

"Where do you think you're going? Has Don Marcelo ever invited you to eat in his private room?"

Tony is upset. Galletano made him remember he was not up to the standard he believes he was.

"I will not eat, just say hello," Tony replies.

"Neither to eat, nor to greet, nor to anything, to that room only enters who Don Marcelo allows and you are not in that group." Galletano responds emphatically.

"Excuse me Galletano, it's that having to wait four hours to ask a question seems abusive to me."

Galletano, with his bully face, and with his usual toothpick in his mouth, responds.

"Well, there is no other. You wait, you leave or ask me."

Tony realizes he will have to wait, so he asks Galletano out of curiosity. Tony takes the picture he had taken with Vittorio and tells him. "I doubt you know this, old man."

When Galletano saw the photo, he paled and gave the photo back as if the photo was burning. "From where do you know this Old Man?

Tony was left with his mouth open; he didn't expect such a reaction. "Do you know him?"

Galletano responds. "That old man came here and said he wanted to talk to Don Marcelo. Since we didn't know who he was, we told him he wasn't here. The old man stood up and went straight to Don Marcelo's office. I stopped him before he came inside and gave him his good taps as usual. When Don Marcelo heard he was Don Vittorio, he almost killed me. As I understand it, that old man comes from the top. I heard he saved Don Marcelo's life. And he even saved my life because he interceded for me so that Don Marcelo would not cut my balls. Don Marcelo took him to his private room, offered him a gala dinner and then I had to take him to the best hotel and take care of him until the other day when he left."

Tony felt mixed emotions. On the one hand, Tony felt betrayed by Caino, as Vittorio had told him, but he felt flattered to think that such a high-level character had set his sights on him to do business. He believed Vittorio would give him great prestige in the organization. Tony waited four hours so he could have a few minutes with Marcelo. Tony enters Marcelo's office and Marcelo tells him. "Whatever you have to tell me, tell me quickly. It's late."

Tony, believing that he will earn points by partnering with Vittorio, takes the photo and shows it to Marcelo, telling him arrogantly. "I think you know this, gentleman."

"Yes, I know him very well. And what do you know about him?" Marcelo answers.

"I know he's a high-level character who's taking refuge here for a while and who has partnered with me to do business." Tony responds with an air of grandeur.

Marcelo takes the photo and breaks it into pieces. "Your stupidity goes beyond what I thought. You know that a superior to you is taking refuge here and you go around showing his photo on the street. Is this how you protect your superiors?"

Tony says. "No Don Marcelo, I'm not doing that."

Marcelo punches the table and responds. "You show the photo to Galletano and now you just show it to me. I doubt he will do business with you, because he will ask about you. He told me he warned you that you have a traitor by your side, but you are such an idiot that you don't see it. He told me he thought that since I had recommended you establish Alberto, you were more intelligent. I think you already know what you wanted; you can leave now."

The airs of grandeur disappeared in Tony, who left the office like a dog with his tail between the legs. "Forgive the inconvenience, Don Marcelo, and thank you for your advice. You have always been a teacher to me. Have a good night."

Tony wasted no time and went straight to call Dino. Dino slept soundly when the phone rang. "Hello."

"Hello Dino, it's me Tony."

"What's the matter, Tony?" You scare me when you call me at 3:30 AM."

"Yes, it's urgent. Vittorio was right. Caino is a traitor. I want you to monitor him, but not alert him. He will not get away with it."

Dino couldn't believe it. He knew Caino personally and had never suspected of him, but he would not contradict his boss for anything in the world.

"Listen boss, old Vittorio tried to communicate with you yesterday all day. Then he contacted me in the afternoon and told me we had to take the goods out of there. I told him that only you could give the order, and that you were coming back this morning."

Tony took a deep breath and slammed the phone's headset three times against the phone booth to vent his frustration.

"Listen Dino, from today on I don't want to hear you say THE OLD VITTORIO. You will call him DON VITTORIO. Tomorrow, you pick up Caino at 10:00A.M. after that, you pick me up to go move that merchandise."

Dino, confused, asks. "Boss, but if Caino is a traitor, we can't use him to move the goods."

"You only do what I ask of you. I know what I am doing." Tony hangs up the phone and then takes the headset and slams it against the phone several times while screaming. "Damn fat man, you're going to pay for this."

The next day, Tony, Dino, and Caino arrive at the warehouse and see that there are two police units in front of the warehouse. Tony thinks the drug has been confiscated and screams.

"Damn, not only do I lose the money, but now they will distrust my abilities."

Tony sees Lieutenant Clark and feels great relief. He thinks the lieutenant is at the scene to make sure that no one steals the drug. Tony gets out of the car and slowly heads towards the lieutenant.

"Hello lieutenant, what a surprise to find you around here, but it's a pleasant surprise because if you're here, that means everything is under control."

The lieutenant understands the double meaning Tony is using and responds.

"This time it is not like that. Some thieves stormed the warehouse last night and took the engines that the business had to send to some customers."

Tony felt like a stab in the chest, but he tries to stay calm. Tony's face is red, and the veins in his neck look like they are going to explode at any moment. "How did something like this happen? He never had problems before."

The lieutenant looks at Tony and tries to understand what is going on, then he replies. "This morning, when they opened the business, they found old Vittorio gagged, his eyes covered and tied in a chair. The old man says that the car that is been hanging around at night was parked at the entrance to the business. The old man went out to investigate, when two hooded men with guns without saying a word forced him into the warehouse and then searched for a long time until they found the specific engines. The old man could not give descriptions of the thieves because they covered their faces and never said a word. The old man gave a full description of the vehicle, including three numbers on the license. It's clear they knew what they were looking for."

Tony is about to faint; his blood pressure is beyond the limits of danger. "Do you think that with the description of the vehicle and three numbers on the license plate, you can find those thieves?"

The lieutenant with an affirmative tone answers him. "Believe me, that will be my priority. The car is a red 1957 Chevy, white roof, white band tires and if we add the three numbers on the plate, it will not take long to find it."

When Tony hears the description of the vehicle, he remembers that Caino's brother had a similar car and immediately looks at Caino. Caino is pale and about to faint.

"No! No! No! That can't be. That's my brother's car. They're setting a trap for me." Screams Caino.

Tony had not only convinced himself that Caino was a traitor, but that he should eliminate him as an example to others. Tony puts his hand on Caino's shoulder and responds.

"I believed you when you told me not to give the list to Vittorio. Isn't it true?"

"Yes, it's true, Don Tony." Caino responds, almost crying.

"You have been by my side for almost ten years, having no problems. Isn't it true?"

"That's totally true." Caino responds, feeling great relief.

"So how do you think I'm going to believe an old man I met yesterday before you? We have to transport the cargo off a boat that awaits us outside the bay, we will bring it to the warehouse and then in that same boat we are going to get rid of Vittorio and I want to give you the honor of doing it."

Caino feels a hunch that Tony is lying but did not dare to refuse, so as not to raise suspicions against him.

"Did you find out about that Vittorio?" Asks Caino

Tony takes his toothpick out of his mouth and responds with a smile. "As you warned me, Don Marcelo doesn't even know who he is. I'm sure no one stole the merchandise, and it's his invention to keep it and then sell it."

Caino is relieved and thought that he will enjoy the elimination of Vittorio. Tony tells Dino and Caino. "You guys wait here. I'll talk to that old man for a moment and then we'll go to get merchandise that is waiting for us outside the bay."

Dino understood that Caino's fate was sealed and that he should stay with Caino and not let him go for anything in the world. Tony enters the warehouse with Lieutenant Clark and sees Vittorio sitting behind the desk.

"Good morning, Don Vittorio."

"I don't know what's good about it." Vittorio answers emphatically.

"I want to apologize for not listening to you before, but I assure you that this traitor is going to speak up and tell me where he has the drug."

Vittorio stands and angrily responds. "I don't know what the fuck you're talking about."

"Don't worry, Don Vittorio Lieutenant Clark is my right hand, and that's why he came immediately when he heard what happened."

Vittorio responds slowly. "I warned you several times, and you didn't listen. Yesterday I tried to talk to you, but you didn't reply. I told Dino that we had to get the merchandise out of here because it was not safe, and he told me that only you could give the order. I took the merchandise and divided it into twelve boxes and then put the boxes in different places in the warehouse. Those who came knew how much it was because they kept searching until they found it all. Tell me if you have any doubt. They came when you were out of town, and they also knew the amount of merchandise that was in the warehouse."

Tony sadly replies. "This more than a loss is a lesson for me, but today a new era begins. This will never happen to us again."

Vittorio raises both hands by moving them from side to side. "No! No! No! I don't work with amateurs."

Tony lowers his voice, and as a plea, he answers. "Please Don Vittorio, I don't want to work with Gregorio. He is an idiot. Not only have I lost a considerable sum of money, but I am also now forced to move more merchandise to recover what I lost. I offer you fifty percent."

Vittorio understood Gregorio was not out of danger if he did not give Tony another chance. Vittorio, pointing his index finger directly at Tony's face, showing that he was in absolute control, responds to him.

"I only accept if you listen to me and tell your lieutenant that my name cannot appear on any police report. I would never have called the police, but that asshole Alberto got scared and called them."

Tony felt great relief. He thought he still made up for all the damage to his reputation and recover the monetary loss. Haughtily, he tells Vittorio.

"That report will never come out of here."

Tony turns around and says to the lieutenant. "Cancel that report. Don Vittorio's name must be kept hidden."

Lieutenant Clark, annoyed, responds. "That's not so easy. Every call is recorded, and I will have to explain to the captain what happened."

Vittorio pours more gasoline on the fire. Vittorio slowly walks towards Tony, has his gaze fixed on him, puts both hands-on Tony's shoulders. Then he says in his ear.

"If that's your strong man, and he has trouble obeying your commands, then you can go fuck yourself and forget that you ever met me."

When Gregorio heard Vittorio and saw Tony's frightened face, he turned around and left behind some shelves, where he put a handkerchief in his mouth so he could hold the laughter. Tony knows he has to show respect, or he will be completely lost. The lieutenant had not heard what Vittorio said because he was making a personal call on the warehouse phone.

Tony asks the lieutenant to hang up the call and to come closer. Tony, seeing that the lieutenant is still on the phone, approaches and hangs up the phone. The lieutenant looks at him in surprise and says.

"What the fuck is wrong with you? I am not your puppet."

Tony felt a cold spreading all over his back. If Lieutenant Clark didn't obey him, that would be the final push that would take him down. Tony gambled because he had nothing more to lose. Tony stands in front of the lieutenant and, in a threatening voice, tells him.

"You could be the lieutenant, but I am your boss. Remember that the one who pays commands, and I have paid you very well. I don't give a damn about those police records. You're going to delete that report right now."

Clark flushes. On his face, it is noticeable that he is about to explode. No one had ever disrespected him in that way, but he understood that if he fights with Tony even if he wins, he could lose his career and end up in jail. Both stared at each other as if in a duel or perhaps a poker game. The young police officer, who was still taking data to finish his report, enters the warehouse to tell the lieutenant that he finished the report.

"Lieutenant, I am going to ask for the case number to give it to Mr. Vittorio, and if you don't need me, I will put myself in service."

The lieutenant responds, annoyed. "Don't ask for any case numbers. Nothing has happened here."

"But lieutenant, and the stolen motors and the blow that Mr. Vittorio had taken to his head?"

The annoying lieutenant replies to him. "It was all a stupid joke they made on the old man and since they had covered his eyes, he tried to run away and hit his head."

The confused young officer responds. "But I talked to the Mr. Vittorio, and he told me."

The lieutenant won't let him finish speaking, punched the counter and yelled at him.

"Are you deaf or idiot? Or a combination of both? I told you that nothing happened and if you mention the subject again, this will be the last day you wear that uniform."

The young officer who had only been in the department for a month and was still on probation paled and was trembling as he tore the report into pieces and threw it in the trash.

"Yes, yes, yes lieutenant, no, nothing has happened. I am leaving and putting myself in service immediately."

Meanwhile, in the parking lot of the shipyard, Caino tried to convince Dino that he was not a traitor. "Dino, you have known me for many years. You know my whole family. In our family, there are no traitors."

Dino's silence increased concern in Caino. Caino separates a little from Dino and Dino asks.

"Where are you going?

"I just want to go to the cafeteria; I am starving."

Dino answers bluntly. "Don Tony said don't move from here."

"It's okay, I will stay here. You can buy me something to eat."

"No, we can't move from here until Don Tony comes back."

Caino's face paled. He understood that if he got on the boat with Tony and Dino, he would not return.

"Okay, we'll wait together. It looks like you had an excellent breakfast, so you don't care that I'm starving."

Dino looks at him and answers. "Who are you going to fool? You have never missed breakfast in your life."

Caino acts as if everything is normal while looking for an opportunity to escape. Taking advantage of Dino's carelessness during the conversation, Caino gets close enough and hits Dino in the jaw with all his strength. Dino falls to his knee is daze, but Caino kicks him in the head with all his strength and Dino is knocked unconscious to the ground. Caino looks for Tony's car keys to flee. Some customers who are leaving the shipyard see when Caino hits Dino and checks his pockets. The young officer coming out of the warehouse hears the customers screaming and runs to see what happens.

The customers are yelling at the officer. "The fat guy hit the guy on the ground, stole something from his pocket and now he's trying to run away in that car."

Caino knew Dino would not wake up for a long time, so he was trying to move the seat back because he could hardly get in the front seat. Caino hears the officer's screams and tries to flee in a hurry. The officer fires hitting the vehicle several times, but does not hit Caino.

The gunfire shocks everyone inside the warehouse and runs to see what happened. The lieutenant sees the young officer in the middle of the parking lot still shooting at the vehicle and yells at him.

"Stop, you're going to kill someone. If you didn't get him when he was close, you will not hit him now this far away."

The young officer, with adrenaline at one hundred percent and eyes almost popping out of his face, points to the witnesses of the incident and responds to the lieutenant.

"They warned me that this thief hit the victim who is on the ground and stole something from his pocket and then fled. The subject is easy to identify, is obese and almost did not fit in the front seat."

"Go after him." The lieutenant orders him.

"How will I go after him if he is gone?"

The angry lieutenant yells at him. "Orders are not to be discussed. Try to find him. I'll take the witnesses' testimonies."

The officer is in chock. He does not know what to do. He doesn't know where the vehicle is heading to. The lieutenant's scream makes him react.

"What the fuck are you waiting for, or quit your job?"

The young officer leaves the shipyard with lights and siren at a high speed. Tony, Lieutenant Clark and Vittorio lift Dino from the ground and take him inside the warehouse. Tony was on the verge of a heart attack. Clark had his blood pressure about to explode, while Vittorio and Gregorio had to pinch themselves to hold the laughter and not be discovered. Tony takes a deep breath and says.

"I know where he's going. You and I will go to his brother's house. You will hide in front of the house. I will stay on your patrol three blocks away. When I hear gunshots, I will take your vehicle to you instantly."

Tony pulls out a gun and gives it to Clark. "This gun is reported stolen. Make sure it has Caino's fingerprints, and he does not survive."

An enraged Clark rejects the gun. "You're wrong about me. I will kill no one. I'm not a murderer. You paid me for information and protection, not for killing."

An enraged Tony replies. "This is different. We are at war. That traitor has all the information necessary to put us behind bars for life. He will not think twice about asking for federal protection and immunity to save his skin while you and I will be in jail for life."

Tony's words were like a kick in the stomach for Clark, but he understood it was true and that if he did not act now, it could be a disaster. Clark takes the gun and says. "I will get rid of the fat whore, but this is over here."

Vittorio intervenes sarcastically. "I congratulate you Tony. You have an exceptional talent for fucking things up. I try to hide, and you were putting me in public records. We have a traitor on the loose, a police shooting in the parking lot, and you're going to fix everything by adding a dead body."

Gregorio had to pinch himself so hard not to laugh that he gave a cry of pain. Tony sadly replies. "We have no alternative. If the traitor betrays us, you would also be discovered."

Tony, Dino, and Clark leave the warehouse, and Tony tells Dino. "You are still stunned, so you are not any good like that. Take a taxi and go home. See you tomorrow."

Inside the warehouse, everyone was celebrating and laughing. Gregorio had his hand bandaged from so many pinches. "They say that laughter rejuvenate, so today I recovered all the years that I lost because of that bandit." Alberto hugs his wife and says. "I told you, love, we would come out of this one and I fulfill it for you."

Lieutenant Clark is hiding near Caino's brother's house and about five minutes later sees Tony's car approaching. Caino is driving slowly, trying to see if anyone is following or waiting for him. Caino goes around the block several times and thinks it's safe to get out. Caino parks the car in front of his brother's house, who is watching him from the second-floor window. Caino gets out of the car and hears his name being called. He turns around and sees Clark pointing a gun at him. Clark fires two shots and Caino falls to the ground, mortally wounded. Benito (Caino's brother) sees his brother on the ground and Clark putting a gun in his brother's hand. Benito doesn't make a noise, because he knows that if he comes out Clark will kill him too. Benito controls his fury, but he can't control his tears. Tony took Clark's patrol car to the scene in record time, got out of the car and mingles with the many curious people who gather in front of the house.

Clark informs the station of what happened and requests the young officer who was handling the call at the shipyard. Captain Kelly, Detective Robert, and the young officer show up at the scene. Clark asks the officer.

"Can you identify the subject?"

The young officer lifts the sheet that covers Caino and responds.

"Yes, that's the same guy who ran away from the scene after hitting and robbing the victim."

Clark haughtily to impress the captain responds.

"If you really love your profession, after twenty-three years of service, you will know where these individuals hang around. The rest was pure luck."

Clark takes out a sheet of paper and gives it to detective Robert.

"For your information, the subject hit the victim and what he took out of his pocket was the keys to the car. The victim is the driver of a customer who was at the business. These thieves steal expensive cars to sell in other states. They are dangerous and would not hesitate to kill. Thank God that I was armed and was faster than him. In that paper you have the witness's information who saw the subject hitting the victim to steal the car. "When I shot him, he fell to the ground, but he still had his weapon in his hand. I kicked his hand for my safety. I copied the weapon's serial number and gave it to the records section. They informed me it was reported stolen two years ago. With this, you can close the case in record time."

The impressed captain congratulates Clark.

"Outstanding. If I had two more like you, the department would run on its own. You deserve a medal and today I will talk to the chief, so that an action like this does not go unnoticed."

CHAPTER TEN

BENITO LOOKS FOR REVENGE

Newspapers published the news of Caino's death with headlines such as "Car thief killed by police." "Witnesses identify the alleged car thief who was killed by the police." Benito, Caino's brother, swore he would take revenge for his brother's death. Benito took on visiting the witnesses and posed as a news investigator to interview witnesses who identified his brother as the car thief. The witnesses corroborated the official version and Benito understood the witnesses did not lie, only that they did not know the reality of what had happened.

Benito goes to the shipyard to see if he can discover something. Benito enters the warehouse and introduces himself.

"Good morning, I'm a reporter and I'm doing an investigation about the execution of Caino, the alleged car thief."

Alberto, Vittorio, and Gregorio looked at each other, but suspected nothing.

"How can we help you?"

Benito responds seriously. "I see inconsistencies in this case."

Like which ones? Alberto answers.

"I think no matter how stupid a thief is, he wouldn't steal a car in a parking lot where there are two police cars."

Alberto looks again at his father and Gregorio, who worry. Alberto does not know what to say, but he sees that the supposed reporter is more passionate about the story than usual. Alberto gambles and tells the supposed reporter.

"My friend, you are the first person to say something coherent about this case. I do not swallow that story either. This is the theme of the day at the shipyard. All the customers do nothing but talk about this case."

Benito gets even more excited and his eyes water. Alberto puts his hand on Benito's shoulder and stares at him and says.

"I would like to help you, but if you are not honest with me, do not count on my help."

Benito sees a ray of light in his quest for revenge but did not say his true identity.

"As I told you, this is a strange case, and it's a great opportunity for me if I get to prove that things didn't go like that."

Alberto moves his head in the affirmative and answers. "Leave me your card and I promise you that if I hear anything, I will let you know right away."

Benito gives Alberto a card, shakes his hand and thanks him. Alberto accompanies him to the parking lot and realizes Benito is driving the cart they told Tony that it was involved in the theft of the drugs. Alberto puts his hand on Benito's shoulder and asks.

"Do you really believe that story is false?"

"I'm sure, buddy."

Alberto returns the card and tells him. "Then I'm sorry, my friend, I don't need those kinds of problems. They could sabotage my business or maybe kill me. I just dedicate myself to work. Forgive me."

Benito flushed and angrily replies. "Who has knowledge of a crime and keeps silent about it, becomes complicit of it."

"You are wrong. I don't keep silent about anything. I just know what I've heard. I also know that no one gets shot twice just because. Maybe he did not steal the car, but I am sure that there is something more to it. Finally, there is a significant difference from the one who keeps silent on his own will or for common sense and the one who keeps silence because got his tongue cut off."

Alberto returns to the warehouse where his father and Gregorio are waiting for him.

"What did you say to the journalist?" Gregorio asks curiously.

"First, I promised to help him, but then I told him I would not get into that trouble, that I didn't want to risk someone would take a revenge against us. I returned his card, and he was very upset."

"Why did you do that, son? He is the right person to use in this fight."

Vittorio replies disenchanted.

"First, he's not a journalist. He is Caino's brother and yes, we are going to use him, but he cannot know that we are using him."

Vittorio sits and sighs. "Oh, my god! This is not for me. During the German occupation, I took part in the struggle, and I was never afraid. That is war not theater acting like now. I would have nothing to lose if they discovered me, but this is different. I fear for you all. I act like a mobster, but inside I'm shitting in my pants out of fear. I have to face them and keep pretending. I don't know how much more I can go on without being discovered."

Gregorio laughs mockingly. "You know, Vittorio, your genuine talent is in theatrical comedy."

Vittorio angrily responds. "Fuck you Gregorio, this is very serious."

Vittorio then addresses his son. "Where the fuck did you get he is Caino's brother? How are we going to use him if you returned the card and told him not to contact you?"

Alberto, undeterred, responds. "It was very simple. His interest in the case goes beyond journalism. It is something personal. When I went out to the parking lot, I saw he was riding in the same vehicle that we described as the suspicious vehicle that prowled the warehouse at night. It was Caino who said we were setting a trap for him because that was his brother's vehicle. We already know who he is and where he lives. When we need to use him, we will simply leave him an anonymous note."

Gregorio bursts into laughter. "You don't bullshit me Alberto, you with your naïve face are worse than them. Where do you get your ideas from?"

Vittorio had been left with his mouth open. He never thought that his son could handle such a dangerous situation with such serenity and simplicity.

Gregorio asks Alberto.

"Son, tell me the truth. Who teaches you all those things? Are you related to that Don Franco in Italy?"

"I have no relation to anyone, and we all know that my dad is Don Franco's friend, not me."

Two months of relative calm passed. The damage to Tony's reputation for having been betrayed and robbed was compensated by Tony having executed the traitor, but the economic damages were not compensated. Tony used his reserve to buy another drug shipment and wanted to make sure he wouldn't have problems this time.

Tony shows up one morning with Dino at the warehouse and meets Gregorio.

"Good morning, Don Tony. How can I help you?"

"I don't think I need to talk to you that all. I need to talk to Don Vittorio." Tony responds contemptuously by fixing his tie and making no eye contact with Gregorio.

Gregorio turns around and screams. "Old man, don't be so lazy and move your ass. Don Tony is looking for you."

Tony stretches out his arm on the counter and grabs Gregorio by the collar of his shirt, pulls him towards him and almost chocking him says. "Listen to me, you piece of shit. Let it be the last time I hear you disrespect Don Vittorio, because I'm going to kick your ass so hard that I am going to hurt your entire family."

Tony didn't get to finish the sentence when Vittorio's scream stopped him.

"What do you do, idiot?"

A frightened Tony immediately let go of Gregorio. "He disrespected you. Did you hear what he said when I called you?"

"Of course, I heard it. I'm not deaf. I asked him to do it. You know things have been boiling around here and the last thing I need is for someone to suspect me. No one is going to suspect an old man who is treated like a dog of being someone wanted or highly related to the mafia. You know what the tense the situation is, but you don't get it. If Don Marcelo is your godfather, I think it's time for him to retire. I will not report him, so I won't tarnish his reputation. You will treat me with all respect when we are alone, but when there are clients present, you will treat me like a dog. Is that clear?"

Tony paled. He had started again with his left foot, no words came out of his mouth.

Vittorio stares at Tony and says. "What now? Besides, stupid, now you are deaf and dumb?"

"Yes, Don Vittorio, and forgive me. You always see beyond. Don Marcelo fell short when he told me you were a person from whom I could learn a lot."

"I'm glad you understand, and I hope you don't forget it. Now I want you to apologize to Gregorio."

Tony flushed, apologizing to the person he had always treated like a rag was a humiliation to him. Tony swallows and takes a deep breath. "Sorry Gregorio. I didn't know that these were orders from Don Vittorio."

Vittorio pushes Gregory aside, puts his hands on the counter, leans forward.

"From today on, when you come here and I am not present, you will treat Gregorio with respect and call him Don Gregorio. If someone sees you humiliating Gregorio, they can think that he is your employee and relate you to me, too. I swear that if they discover me, I will cut your balls. I already have enough with the little asshole that is my boss, which, by the way, it was you who placed him here."

Vittorio stares at Tony, who looked like a mummy. After thirty seconds passed and saw that Tony was still in shock, Vittorio breaks the silence.

"Are you going to tell me what you came in for, or have you already forgotten?"

Tony takes a deep breath again and responds.

"I came to inform you that the suppliers will give me a second shipment. This will be double, to replace the loss of the first. We need twice as much space to store the goods and we have to dispose of the goods in at the least five days."

"When does the merchandise arrive?"

"I don't have an exact date." Tony replies.

Vittorio moves his head from side to side and responds. "We've already started badly. You just told me I need twice as much space. I have to prepare the warehouse in case the idiot of Alberto passes by. I need at least three days in advance."

Tony takes a deep breath, moves his head and responds. "I promise you I will do my best to give you three days in advance."

Vittorio responds in a low tone, but as if he were talking to an employee. "If you don't give me three days in advance, don't even think you're going to bring that shit here. You are used to failure, but I am not."

Tony takes a deep breath; he had never felt so humiliated. "It will be as you say, I promise you."

Dino hadn't spoken a word. He only listened, but it surprised him how Vittorio humiliated Tony. When Tony and Dino got into their car to leave. Tony unbuttons his tie in a hurry and punches the car door to vent his anger. Dino, trying to calm him down, tells him.

"I understand that the old man is connected to those above, but we can't let him treat us that way. If this reaches the ears of others after the fiasco we had with the theft of the drug, we will lose respect. I think it would be better not to do business with him, plus it's costing us fifty percent."

Tony, rubbing his forehead with his right hand, replies. "It's my fault for not paying attention to him. That he does business with us helps us to improve the image. I offered him fifty percent to get him more interested in the business. We need to recover our prestige and our money. He is passing through. He will be my letter of introduction when he returns to Italy."

Dino shrugs his shoulders and responds. "Then we will have to put up with it, because I fill like grabbing him by the neck and make him swallow his stupidities."

Tony stares at Dino and replies. "I assure you that anyone else who dares to treat me like this ends up at the bottom of the sea with four blocks tied up around the neck."

The business was so busy that they couldn't meet until late at night in the cafeteria where they were having dinner. Vittorio was worried because he became more and more entangled with Tony.

"You think it's easy for me to play this role? I fear that at any moment something will go wrong, and we will all pay the consequence of my mistake. It terrifies me to carry that guilt."

Gregorio tries to calm him down. "You're doing great, even I'm believing it."

Lucia represses him. "This is not a game. If we're in this, it's because of you, so put a little more seriousness into this."

Gabriela puts her plate aside and asks. "What is your plan now, Alberto? I'm sure Tony will be very cautious, and it won't be so easy this time."

Alberto does not respond and continues to bite a chicken leg. Vittorio throws a piece of bread at him, hitting him on his head. "Talk. She asked you a question."

Alberto picks up the bread that his father threw at him from the table and takes a bite of it, then takes some wine and responds. "Starting tomorrow, I will go out on the motorcycle to observe all the movements of Lieutenant Clark. We must know what his routine is. We will pass by Caino's brother's house at dawn and leave him a message."

Gregorio asks. "How will we leave him a message if we don't even know his name?"

"That doesn't matter. We'll just wait for his response."

"Brilliant!" Gregorio replies.

"Now we're going to get exposed by Caino's brother."

"None of that." Alberto answers.

"Today, late at night, you and Gabriela will stop by his house and leave a message on the windshield of his car. Gabriela is the one who must leave the message because he saw you in the warehouse, but it is preferable that no one sees us."

That night, with no one seeing her, Gabriela leaves the message on the windshield of Benito's car. Benito in the morning discovers the envelope on his windshield and curiously reads it:

"If you want to do justice for the murder of your brother, leave a garbage bag on top of the trunk of your car tonight. Then I will communicate to you when and how at the right time. But if you want Lieutenant Clark not to pay for his cowardly crime, do nothing, and I will do it myself in memory of my friend. I will just pass by tonight from 6 PM to 8 AM and take your answer as definitive."

Benito felt chills on his back. Someone else knew about this crime. That person, although remained anonymous, will help him take revenge. Benito was so thirsty for revenge that he never thought that he might be just another victim too. That day, Benito returns home early and fills a garbage bag and puts it in the trunk of his car. His curiosity was such that he prepares his dinner next to the window and starts watching who passes by. About two hours later, a neighbor sees the garbage bag in the trunk of Benito's car and takes it to throw it away. From his window he yells at him. "Don Augusto, don't bother and leave it there. I am waiting to see if the one who put it there will come back with more garbage to break his neck."

Augusto looks out the window and answers. "I understand. A lack of respect like that deserves a lesson."

Benito stands guard at the window, observes everyone who was not familiar to him and passed by his house. Benito gets up to go to the bathroom for a moment and when he returns, he sees another neighbor taking the garbage bag. Benito runs in a hurry. "Dona Carmen don't bother, I throw it out."

"Son, I thought you had forgotten. It's not a nuisance for me. I will throw it out."

Benito is angry. "No, that is my fucking garbage and I want to throw it away myself."

The frightened old lady drops the garbage bag to the ground, then enraged kicks it and the bag opens, scattering all the garbage on the sidewalk. "Poorly educated, ungrateful. Now pick up your shit."

Benito clenches his fists, closes his eyes and takes a deep breath. Benito picks up the garbage and puts it in his bag. He never thought that a simple task like that would be so difficult for him. Benito puts the garbage bag on the trunk and sits in a chair next to his car to make sure no one else takes the bag from him. There were so many cars and strange people that passed that Benito could not be sure if they received the message, so he waits until 6 AM. as the message said. Late at night, Benito could not stay awake anymore, so he held the bag with one hand to make sure that no one was going to take it. In the early hours of the morning, a homeless drunk sees Benito asleep and holding a bag as if holding something of value. The drunk, without thinking twice, carefully removes the bag and runs away on his tiptoe with his supposed treasure.

Benito is awakened by the cane of Dona Carmen. "Do you think I'm afraid of you? I told my husband what you did to me yesterday. Get ready, he is going to come talk to you. Do not think that because he is in a wheelchair, he will let you get away with something like this."

Benito ignored Doña Carmen. He realized he is missing the garbage bag and screamed. "My God, it can't be. What do I do now?"

Benito takes the chair and is going inside his home, while the old woman yelled at him. "You are running away like an asshole when I told you that my husband was coming, you coward."

For two weeks, Alberto, Vittorio and Gregorio took turns following Clark and writing his movement pattern during his working hours. Alberto noticed that usually at ten PM, Clark would visit the restaurant "Jack" then take Washington Road to return to the police station where he stayed for two hours and then return to patrol.

Once again, the family gathers, and Alberto informs them.

"I have a plan to get rid of the drug shipment that's coming and Lieutenant Clark at the same time."

All intrigued look at each other, Alberto had not informed them of his plan.

Alberto addresses his wife. "How are we doing financially?"

"We finished paying the hospital expenses and we have three thousand dollars in the bank."

Alberto shakes his head in worry. "That is not enough for us. We need fifteen thousand dollars. Take out a loan or take out a line of credit on the business for fifteen thousand dollars."

Lucia opens her eyes in amazement. "Did you go crazy? We have a year of working just to pay expenses and now we are going to pawn again. Do you plan to pay for the drug and then throw it into the sea? That will not solve the problem. On the contrary, it will ruin us."

Alberto smiles and replies. "No love, that's not the idea, but it will cost us about ten thousand dollars."

So why do you want Fifteen Thousand? Gregorio asks.

"So that no one can tie up the dots that lead to us." Alberto answers.

"Well, I don't agree, we can't continue to work like animals and live like beggars, that's not fair." Gregorio responds angrily.

"Very good. Do any of you have a plan?" Alberto asks.

Everyone looks at each other and no one says a word. Gabriela stands in front of her husband and asks him. "What's your plan?"

"No, I don't have any plans."

Gabriela angrily replies. "Then shut up and cooperate. You've screwed up enough."

Gregorio opens his eyes. On his face there was shame and anger, but deep down, he knew his wife was right. Gregorio gets up and responds.

"If I don't have the right to have an opinion, then what do I do here?"

Gregorio tries to leave, and Alberto stops him. "If you were a hindrance to us, we wouldn't be doing all this. You are part of the family and in the family, we are all important. Would you be willing to do the same for me?"

Gregorio was moved by Alberto's words. "You can rest assured I would not hesitate for a second to give my life to any of you. It hurts me a lot and I recognize that all this has been my fault."

Tears ran down Gregorio's cheeks. Alberto hugs him, and Lucia joins him. Gabriela feels embarrassed and joins the embrace, asking her husband for forgiveness. They all end up in a family hug, making a circle. Vittorio sings "O bella ciao" and everyone sings and dances in a circle together.

Suddenly, Gregorio screams. "Enough is enough. What's the plan?"

The group separates, and Alberto responds. "Tomorrow, Lucy will get the money and buy three flashlights. Lucy, make sure they are the most powerful you can get. Gregorio will have to look for an old truck. You will pay half to secure the purchase and you will tell them that when you have the rest of the money, you will pick it up. This way, no one will see the truck in our parking lot. The rest I'll tell you later. This is it for now."

CHAPTER ELEVEN

DEATH OF LIEUTENANT CLARK

It had been three weeks when one morning Tony and Dino show up at the warehouse. Gregorio hands an order to a customer and says. "Good morning, Don Tony. How can I help you?"

Tony replies. "Good morning, Don Gregorio. I placed an order with the old man who works here, and he has never come back to me."

Gregorio turns and screams. "Old man, bring your ass over here and take care of your shit."

Vittorio comes out downcast and says. "Good day Don Tony, I am so sorry."

Tony responds arrogantly. "Do you have my order?"

"Sorry Don Tony, but I need three days."

Tony fixes his tie, slaps the counter, and responds.

"Well, from today you have three days, I want it in three days or I will kick your ass so hard that you will land back in Italy."

The customer who was in the warehouse took it personally.

"Who the fuck do you think you are to treat this old man that way? Don't you have a father? If that man was my family, I would make you swallow your rudeness."

Tony is surprised. He didn't expect that reaction from the client. Dino sees the client has not only challenged his boss, but has clenched fists to fight if Tony makes any moves. Dino stands between Tony and the client. He thinks he will intimidate the client.

"Ah! so brave with the old man, but a coward with others. You need a gorilla to defend you."

The client was a man in his sixties who had been known for his great punch as a boxer during his youth. The customer puts the order on the counter and takes off the glasses. Vittorio and Gregorio look at each other, and Gregorio whispers to Vittorio. "This is getting better and better every day."

Dino mockingly tells him. "You'd better put on your glasses, so you won't have the excuse that you didn't see it coming."

Dino has not finished the sentence when the client gives him a punch that leaves him lying on the ground unconscious.

At that precise moment, Alberto enters and sees the client standing with his fists closed and Dino lying on the ground. "What's happening here?"

The client recognizes Alberto and responds. "I didn't know that you would allow anyone to humiliate your employees. This is the last time I set foot here."

"What are you talking about, Don Genaro? Please explain."

The angry client tells Alberto what happened, and Alberto responds.

"You are wrong Don Genaro; I will never allow something like this in my business. I have a father and whoever disrespects him has to deal with me. Gregorio, you were the one who started with disrespect. You immediately apologize to Don Vittorio, and if I find out that this happens again, you will be fired, even if you are my father-in-law."

Gregorio acts as if he is sorry and responds. "Sorry, Alberto."

"Not to me. Apologize to Don Vittorio right now."

Gregorio lowers his head and looks towards Vittorio, and, trying to contain the laughter, he says.

"Excuse me, Vittorio, it will not happen again."

"It's not Vittorio, it is Don Vittorio. Am I clear?"

"You're right. Excuse me, Don Vittorio."

Dino gets up from the floor and still dizzy looks at Tony. Dino sees that Tony's face is pale, not so much because of the fight, but because he had caused another problem in front of Vittorio.

Dino whispers to Tony. "You'd better apologize before he tells you to apologize."

Tony replies. "First dead, before apologizing to this asshole."

Alberto turns toward Tony and Tony says. "You're absolutely right. I think I should apologize too, but I want to clarify that I was joking with him. I will never disrespect Vittorio."

Alberto raises his right hand to Tony as a sign for him to stop and tells Don Genaro.

"I want to apologize to you on behalf of the business. I assure you, an incident like this will never happen again. I am happy that there are people who stand up to injustices. You have all my respect and here you will always have an unconditional friend."

The client is moved and shakes hands tightly with Alberto. "You are an example that the youth is not lost in this country."

Tony is relieved to see that the client has calmed down, and he thinks the incident is over. Everything fell apart when he hears. "A moment Don Genaro. These gentlemen must also apologize to you. I do not allow disrespect from employees or customers."

Tony and Dino flushed but did not respond.

"I can't force you to apologize, but if I don't listen to your apologies, then you can leave, and you won't be welcome in my business anymore. I will return your money, and nothing has happened here. Mr. Tony, I appreciate what you have done for me, but you decide."

Tony and Dino, as elementary school children say at the same time.

"Excuse me, Don Vittorio, it won't happen again."

"Very good, but the apology is with Don Genaro." Alberto answers.

Tony felt a dagger had been stuck in his chest, that was much more than he could bear. Tony prepares to send Alberto to hell, but sees that Vittorio is staring at him and slouching his head as if to say "YES" he orders him to apologize. Tony takes a deep breath again and responds.

"As I said earlier, you are right, and I apologize not only to Don Vittorio, but to you, Don Genaro."

Tony turns to Dino and says. "Dino, you must also apologize to Don Genaro."

Dino looks down and, without making eye contact, says. "I offer you my sincere apology, Don Genaro."

Genaro looks at him, he moves his head and responds. "I know you're not sincere, but you've received enough for today."

Dino and Tony are sitting in their car without saying a word. Tony is humiliated and worried. Dino is in pain and humiliated. Dino breaks the silence.

"I hate more and more to come to this place, it's as if nothing we do goes right. Won't it be better to forget about these people?"

Tony responds almost without strength. "As I told you earlier, that old man is our ticket to the big leagues. I have already lost enough money and endured humiliations. I can't throw everything away. Let's endure a little longer and we will be victorious. We will recover the lost money and raise our status in the organization. I swear I didn't lack the desire to put a bullet between Genaro's eyebrows and to kick Alberto's ass."

Inside the warehouse, Alberto, Gregorio and Vittorio kept laughing and making fun of Tony and Dino. Alberto tells them. "We already know that the drug arrives in three days. Tonight, we will go out to test the flashlights. Gregorio tomorrow morning, you will buy the truck and be sure to reinforce the front bumper so that it can survive a strong crash. Tonight, you and Gabriela will put a note on Benito's vehicle."

That night Gregorio and Gabriela passed by Benito's house, leaving an envelope on the windshield. When Benito gets out in the morning, he sees the envelope; he takes it and looks around, but he sees nothing out of the ordinary. Benito thought it had all been a mockery of Clark. Benito takes the envelope, opens it and reads:

"If you still want to avenge your brother's death, I wait for you tomorrow at nine forty PM. at Washington Road, exactly four miles north of the restaurant Jack, park your car and wait for directions. If you change your mind, just don't come."

Benito was hesitant. This could be a plan by Clark to eliminate him. Benito looked for his pistol and stayed armed from that moment on. The day came and they all have the adrenaline rushed to the maximum. That night, Alberto set his plan in motion. They loaded into the bed of the truck six large sacks full of drugs and a bag with ten thousand dollars in cash. Lucia dressed in men's clothes and covered her hair with a cap. Alberto post Lucia in Washington Road one mile north of the restaurant, then post Gregorio one mile north of Lucia and his father with the truck one mile north of Gregorio. Vittorio has the truck on the side of the road, heading south, which is the opposite direction from which Lieutenant Clark will come from. His plan was to provoke a chase and as soon as Lucia saw him approaching, she would signal Gregorio by turning the lights off and on three times, and so would Gregorio to Vittorio.

Benito attended the appointment. He knew he could die if it was a trap, but he could not live with the guilt that, for his cowardice, the assassination of his brother was unpunished.

Benito arrives at the place and parks his car next to the road. He sees a truck with a reinforced double defense, with the engine on and a man inside. His instinct makes him stay inside the car, pull out his gun, and be alert to any strange movement. Vittorio gets out of the truck and approaches Benito. Vittorio wears black and has a ski mask covering his face. Benito points the gun at him and tells him. "Don't come any closer or I shoot you."

Vittorio raises both arms. He holds a piece of paper in his right hand. Benito recognizes the modus operandi and keeps aiming, but calmer. Vittorio gives him the paper and gives him the flashlight to read:

"Lieutenant Clark will come at full speed chasing a motorcycle heading north. We will go south in the truck. When the motorcycle passes us, we will change lanes and approach the police car head on. Clark can hit us or throw himself to the side, but he will crash into the pine trees along the road. Then we will put sacks of drugs in the trunk of his patrol car, the back seat of the patrol car, and a bag of money next to him. If Clark does not die in the accident, he will go to jail for many years.

If you have a suitable set of balls, you will drive the truck.

If you have only one ball, you can go in as a passenger.

But if you have ornaments balls, then leave and I will avenge the death of your brother by myself."

Enraged, Benito finishes reading and responds. "I have balls to give you and to fill the bed of your fucking truck."

Without a second thought, Benito gets into the truck. Vittorio gets on the passenger and gives Benito a pair of gloves, and signals him to put it on. Vittorio takes his flashlight and signals to Gregorio that they are ready. Gregorio gives a signal to Lucia, who gives her husband a signal. Alberto positions himself in the parking lot, waiting for Clark to leave the restaurant. Lieutenant Clark leaves the restaurant and goes to his patrol car. Alberto wears a cap and glasses to avoid been recognized. He throws a stone at lieutenant Clark, hitting him on the back, and flees at full speed north on Washington Road. Clark enraged, knows that Washington Road is a straight road and without traffic, he will have no difficulty catching up the motorcycle. Intending to run him over with his patrol car, he gets into his patrol and starts chasing Alberto at full speed. Alberto gives the signal to Lucia by turning off and on his lights three times. Lucia gives the signal to Gregorio that the chase is on. Gregorio quickly turns, giving the signal to Vittorio. Vittorio receives his signal and slaps with his two hands on the dashboard of the truck and signals Benito to move forward in a hurry.

Benito lowers the throttle to the maximum, and the truck shuts down. Vittorio made a cry, breaking the rule of not speaking a word in front of Benito. Benito tried to start the truck in a hurry, with his right hand on the truck key, his foot on the accelerator and with his left hand on the steering wheel.

"Start, you son of a bitch, start."

Everyone is nervous. Lucia sees Alberto passing by at full speed and a moment later, the patrol car passes by with the lights on at a faster speed than Alberto. Lucia breaks down in tears, knowing that at that speed, this will be over soon. Alberto feels the engine of the patrol and worries. Alberto passes Gregorio at his maximum speed and four seconds later, the patrol passes that almost knocked him down with the wind of the speed it was carrying. Gregorio doesn't see the lights of the truck and starts jumping like a madman while screaming. "Where is the fucking truck? Where is Vittorio?"

Alberto despair and already prepared for the worst, closes his eyes and entrusts himself to God.

Alberto hears a big rumble; he doesn't know what has happened. He looks back and doesn't see the patrol car. Alberto does not understand what happened, but he knows that the patrol is not following him anymore. Alberto doesn't understand, if he didn't see any trucks, then why Clark stopped chasing him. Alberto stops and returns. He knows that his wife and Gregorio are on the road, and he fears for their safety. Alberto returns and sees the patrol car smashed against an enormous pine tree. Alberto sees that his father and Benito are lowering the sacks from the truck and continues as planned on his motorcycle to pick up Lucia.

Benito had started the truck and drive at full speed and only turned on the lights when he saw the motorcycle pass. Alberto, in his despair, never saw the truck which was dark, the road was black, and he had closed his eyes, entrusting himself to God at the precise moment when the truck passed by him.

Benito was screaming. "Damn coward, I wanted to crash with you, but you ran away."

Benito and Vittorio carry one sack each and put it in the trunk of the patrol car, then a second trip with two more sacks. On the third trip, Vittorio picks up the money bag and throws it next to Clark. When he returns to the truck, Vittorio gives Benito the last bag and asks him to take it to the patrol car. Benito gladly takes the bag and goes to the patrol car. Benito could not control himself. "You son of a bitch, if you don't die when you get out of jail, I'll kill you."

Benito's joy was so great that he did not realize that Vittorio had left with the truck. Benito screams. "Son of a bitch, come back don't leave me here."

Benito rushes to the road and realizes that it was too late to run after the truck. Suddenly, he sees Vittorio has left him a small bicycle lying on the road for him. Benito gets on the bike and becomes an Olympic cyclist, traveling in record time half a mile to his car. Benito was happy when he saw his car. He thought that besides having abandoned him, his car would be stolen. Benito hurriedly stuffed the small bicycle into the trunk and left in a hurry.

Vittorio picked up Gregorio in the truck and everyone met in the warehouse, where Gabriela was waiting for them. Gabriela burst into tears when she saw them all arrive safe and sound. Gabriela and Lucia went to the cafeteria to prepare something to eat while Alberto, Vittorio, and Gregorio put the last part of the plan to work. The plan was to throw the rest of the drugs into the sea, then dismantle the truck and throw it into the sea as well. The next day was Saturday, and the business was closed, so he had time to throw away the drug, dismantle much of the truck and get rid of it.

Lieutenant Clark was found four hours after the accident. They rushed to the hospital but died later that day. The news spread like an uncontrollable fire. The radio and newspapers kept commenting on it. Speculation was that the lieutenant was involved in drug trafficking and was on the run from other drug traffickers when he lost control of his vehicle, that the lieutenant could outwit those who were chasing him but found death in the attempt. That was the only reasonable hypothesis to explain the ten thousand dollars in cash found next to him.

Tony was at home having breakfast when he got a call from Dino.

"What happens Dino? It's Saturday and too early. Don't you have nothing to do in your house?"

Dino responds. "You haven't heard the news? We have a big problem, bigger than the previous one."

Tony does not know what it is, but if it is worse than the previous, it must be serious. He is about to faint. Tony sits on a chair next to the phone. He is afraid to ask what has happened. Dino asks. "Boss, are listening to me? Are you there?"

"Yes, I am listening to you. I just need a moment to assimilate what you have to tell me."

Dino responds. "Clark was the rat. Now it all makes sense."

Tony opens his eyes and reddens. What! Was Clark also a rat? Where did you get that? Tony responds by punching the wall.

"Yes boss, Clark and Caino stole the drug from us. Clark did not want to share the profits anymore and sowed the evidence against Caino. Clark then eliminated Caino to keep all the loot. I will pick you up as soon as possible to see how much merchandise we had left in the warehouse."

It was Saturday, and Vittorio was alone in the warehouse. It was expected Tony would show up at the warehouse as soon as he received the news. Tony and Dino arrive at the shipyard at full speed and get out of the car, running towards the warehouse. Tony and Dino bang hard at the door constantly. Vittorio takes his time to open.

"What way to knock is that? What is the emergency? I can only sleep in the mornings on Saturdays and Sundays, but I can see that even that is impossible."

Vittorio was exhausted from being up the entire night, but Tony thought it was normal because Vittorio had just gotten up.

"Forgive me, Don Vittorio. I need to know how much merchandise is left?"

Vittorio stares at him and replies.

"What do you mean, how much is left? What the fuck is wrong with you? It will be better for you to explain yourself, because I will not put up with your stupidity."

Tony could not hide his helplessness and bewilderment.

"No, Don Vittorio, that's what I need to know. How much merchandise do we have left?"

Vittorio responds calmly. "Nothing. You took it all yesterday. I think it was stupid to take that merchandise out during the afternoon. A risk like that is totally unnecessary, but coming from you, nothing surprises me anymore."

Tony takes off his hat and throws it on the ground, then takes off his cloak and also throws it on the ground. Vittorio looked at him with a surprised face to play his role, but inside, he laughed out loud.

"Tell me what the fuck is going on. Your lieutenant came and said that you gave the order to move the goods immediately. I told him it wasn't a good idea to do it in the afternoon that it was better to do it at night. Clark replied you wanted the merchandise out of here before ten o'clock at night. I told him to look for a truck to take a single trip. He replied no, that no one would suspect his patrol vehicle, and that those were your orders. Now explain to me what the fuck is going on."

Tony, embarrassed, replies. "Clark stole the merchandise from us."

Vittorio responds indifferently. "He did not steal it from us. He stole it from you. I'm not an asshole. When you proposed the business, I was tempted to invest, but I told you that you had a traitor, that's why I didn't invest. When you told me you would double the investment, I didn't invest either, because as in real life, when you see a rat, it is because there are a hundred more that you have not seen.

That was your trusted man, your trump card. I hope you will bring me Clark's balls in a small box."

Tony is destroyed. He lowered his head and said. "You are wise. You are right, one sees a rat. It is because there must be a hundred more that haven't been seen."

Dino got serious. He didn't like his boss repeating that phrase; he felt reflected in it. Vittorio seized the moment and says. "What's the matter Dino don't you agree with it?"

"Yes, I think it's true, but I'm not a rat."

Vittorio moves his head from side to side. "I have not said that you are a rat, but neither was Caino a rat, nor was the lieutenant a rat."

Tony tries to change the conversation and says.

"The good part is that rat's life is short, and God always does justice. I can't bring you Clark's balls, because he's already dead. Apparently, the same ones with whom he used to betray us betrayed him. In the end, he received what he deserved. He couldn't enjoy the money he stole from us." Vittorio responds worriedly.

"I hope Clark's investigation won't lead them to us. If I have to run away from here, this would bring us problems."

Tony responds. "No, no one can get to us through Clark. I know I could not show you what I can do, and I have only caused upsets. I will not bother you anymore. I will show you I can get up and overcome any problem. I had negotiated a third drug shipment counting on the money I would earn on this one that was stolen from us. I will not give up. I will seek funding and bring the third shipment."

Vittorio asks. "What are you talking about? That's not a thing the bank can finance for you. Only the mafia can finance you and after this fuck up, I doubt anybody will lend you the money."

Tony moves his head and responds.

"I know, but this time I can't fail. Dino is not a stranger; he is family, and this warehouse has turned out to be a safe place. The drug has been lost, but not because it was unsafe here. Between Dino,

Gregorio, and I will do this operation. You will see that I can fall, then rise and succeed." Vittorio convinced that no one would finance Tony's responds.

"I'll be a spectator. Good luck to you."

Vittorio turns around, slams the door, and goes to sleep.

The news that Tony wasn't given up fell to everyone like a bucket of cold water, but they thought it would be impossible for Tony to get the money to finance the purchase of a third drug shipment.

CHAPTER TWELVE

TONY ASKS FOR A LOAN

Tony asks Don Venancio for a loan. Don Venancio was fifty-five years old, medium height, muscular, and curly gray hair. He was one of the cruelest in the entire organization. His specialty was to give short-term loans with very high interest. His collection team comprised four thugs who loved torture, and quite a few of those who fell behind in the payments did not survive. Don Venancio was already aware of the stumbles Tony had had lately. Vittorio had asked Marcelo to spread the news about Tony's failures. Marcelo, as he did not like Tony, made sure that everyone found out without knowing where the news had come from.

Tony shows up at Don Venancio's car sales office, of which more than half were cars stolen in other states. Tony extends his hand to greet him. "Good morning, Don Venancio."

Venancio doesn't get up to shake Tony's hand, just looks at him and tells him.

"Tony, if you're around here, it's because you need something. Tell me what you offer, and I will tell you if I am interested."

Tony sees Venancio has left him with his right hand extended, so he crosses his hand, pushing the sleeve of his jacket off the left hand as if he wanted to see the time.

"Oh, my God! I didn't know it was so late. I will be brief, because I have an important appointment in two hours."

Venancio responds emphatically. "Then get to the point. I am working."

Tony knew Venancio was a pedantic and uneducated man, but he had never treated him that way. Tony understood that his two failures had eroded his respect in the organization.

"I offer you the opportunity to diversify your business. I am negotiating a shipment of a commodity that is increasing in demand. We will not have to distribute; the buyer takes care of everything. If you are interested, you can invest with me. We are talking about tripling the investment, that is a three hundred percent profit. The buyer examines the quality of the merchandise and if he approves it, he pays us right there and he takes care of the rest. Where can you make money that easy?"

Venancio reclines in his chair, rubs his chin, and asks. "What if the buyer does not approve of the quality of the drug?"

Tony smiles. "It's a serious supplier. I have bought two orders from him previously and his quality is excellent. That same question I asked him the first time I did business with him. His answer was that he guaranteed his merchandise and if for some reason I am not satisfied, I just return it."

Venancio moves his head in approval and says.

"Very well, Tony, I know that's the business of the future. The police are making my life more and more difficult. What do you want from me?"

Tony was relieved. If Venancio finances the drug, he would be back in the game. "You just have to invest, and we split the profit in half. I take care of everything."

Venancio looks at him seriously and responds. "Tony, you are an idiot, but I am not. You want me to pay for the drug and then divide the profits. You want to make money with my money."

Tony becomes offended and responds. "I have all the contacts and I do all the work. Is that worthless?"

Venancio points his finger at him mockingly replies. "It would be worth if you managed to do the business, but already two of your operations ended in failure. I don't want to take the risk. I will lend you the money. If you're so sure you're making three hundred percent, then you wouldn't mind paying one hundred and fifty interest."

Tony opens his arms as a question. "That's the same thing I proposed to you."

Venancio laughs. "No Tony, it's not the same. If I invest and something goes wrong, I can't charge you. If I lend you the money, you have to pay me whether it goes wrong or not. You take it or leave it."

Tony, in desperation, responds. "Okay, I'm sure of what I have therefor I'm not worried about that high interest."

Venancio asks again. "How much do you need?"

Tony replies. "This operation requires fifty thousand dollars."

Venancio stands up, puts both hands on the desk, and leans forward.

"Listen to me Tony, you know I don't play when it comes to collecting. I'm going to treat you like any other customer. If you are one day late, I want your house. The next month I want your restaurant. The third month, I break both your legs and the fourth month, I shoot you in the forehead."

Tony confidently replies. "I know you are relentless when it comes to collecting. I would never come to see you if I had a doubt. Just remember that I offered you the opportunity to invest, and you refused. Then, when you see how profitable this business is and you want to invest, I won't offer you the same percentage."

Venancio answers. "Okay, come back in three days. I will have the money and the contract for you to sign."

Everyone had gathered at Alberto's house to throw a farewell party for Vittorio. They never thought Tony would get financing to buy the drug. Vittorio lifts his glass to toast.

"I toast to you all, who have accepted me and cared for my son as if he was yours. I leave in peace, knowing you all are out of danger.

I want to return as soon as possible with my wife for the baptism of a grandson or granddaughter."

Gregorio raises his cup and says. "You don't know how much we will miss you. We get used to having you among us. Thanks to you, we have been able to get out of this nightmare."

Vittorio responds. "It wasn't me who achieved this, it was Alberto. Without Albert, I don't know what we would have done."

Gregorio laughs and says. "At first I thought he was a mobster, but now, I have no doubt."

Gabriela responds. "I also at first thought he was an asshole, but now, I have no doubt either."

Lucia intervenes. "Mother, please don't talk about Alberto like that. He doesn't deserve those comments."

Gabriela laughs. "No daughter, I'm not talking about Alberto. I'm talking about your father."

Everyone laughs except Gregorio. "Hey, hey, more respect."

Lucia says. "Don Vittorio don't go to work this week. Take the opportunity to go to know New York."

Vittorio replies. "Thank you, Lucy, but what am I going to do alone in that city? I prefer to be with you and help in any way I can. I will miss the seviche prepared by the Peruvian cook. That is not something I have in Italy. Also remember that the last operation cost us ten thousand dollars."

On Monday morning, Gregorio and Vittorio were in the warehouse when they saw Tony and Dino coming in. "Good morning, Don Gregorio. How are you?"

Gregorio couldn't believe it. Tony is back. He looks at Vittorio, who is also as overwhelmed as he is. Vittorio looks at Gregorio, who doesn't know what to do. Vittorio beckons Gregorio to attend Tony. He thinks maybe it could be something else unrelated to smuggling. Gregorio answers.

"Good morning, Don Tony. How can I help you?"

Tony responds contemptuously. "Pay attention to what I'm going to tell you. I need you to prepare space. This time will come triple what came last time. I don't want to bother Vittorio, plus he might leave, and I must train you for the future."

Gregorio thought that when Clark died, Tony would not have the power to blackmail him, so he confronted him.

"You did business with Vittorio and pushed me aside. Look for someone else to solve your problem, plus you said I was stupid, and you haven't been very smart either."

Tony couldn't contain the anger and grabbed him through the counter by the neck.

"Who the fuck do you think you are? Do you want to see how, when Vittorio lives, I burn this shit with you inside? Do you forget what I am capable of? I want you to know that because Lieutenant Clark is no longer with us, that does not mean that I do not have more contacts in the police. If you refuse to work with me, I swear to you that when Vittorio returns to Italy, you will be a dead man."

Vittorio tells Tony. "Let him go."

Tony lets go of Gregorio and sarcastically fixes the collar of Gregorio's jacket. Vittorio stands in front of Gregorio and tells him.

"What's the matter Gregorio? You look like you've seen a ghost? I want you to know that I am aware of your and Tony's secret. If you do not do what Tony asks you, he will denounce you and I can serve as a witness. I will say that you yourself told me you provoked the fire that ended the lives of the three sons of Mr. O'Connor."

Gregorio was so surprised that Tony believed Vittorio was serious. Tony felt great relief. He saw in Vittorio the ally he needed in those moments. Vittorio tells Gregorio.

"Now go away. I have to talk to Tony. Don't be brave in front of me again because I'm going to kick you in the ass so hard that's going to hurt your whole family. I don't give a damn if you're the father of Alberto's wife."

Gregorio leaves, and Vittorio tells Tony. "Listen Tony, I don't want people to relate me to you and just remember that you were a failure. Comments like that affect my reputation. I also want you to train Gregorio so that when I am not here, you can go on alone without me, but I will direct this operation. Everything should be done as I tell you, but Gregorio must think you are in charge. Is that clear?"

Tony gives Vittorio a firm handshake. "It will be as you say, and you will not regret your decision. This time there will be no failures."

Vittorio moves his head and responds. "I've heard that before. I will not take the risk of you screwing it up and getting me involved. You have to tell me everything, so there is no surprise."

Tony tells in great detail the meeting he had with Don Venancio and how Venancio had agreed to lend him the money, then arrogantly comments.

"As you can see, Don Venancio is not a novice in these matters and did not think twice about accepting my offer."

Vittorio stares at Tony and asks. Did you tell him about me?

"No Don Vittorio, of course not. He knows nothing about you. Do you know him?"

Vittorio responds by pointing his finger at him. "Those below you should know only two levels above them, but those above you should know everyone below them. Now come back in two days and I will tell you if I approve of your plan."

Tony bewildered replies. "I gave my word to Don Genaro that we will do business."

Vittorio had a notebook in his hand where he had written the orders to be delivered. Vittorio throws the notebook at Tony, hitting him on the head.

"Don't contradict me. It's going to be my way or the highway. You have no business with him unless you take the money. If he tries to pressure you, then I will take care of him."

Tony feels protected by Vittorio's attitude and what matters least to him is that Vittorio has thrown the notebook over his head. He takes it as a father's scolding. "It will be as you say, Don Vittorio. The day after tomorrow, I will be here just out of respect and normality, because I know you will approve this operation."

Everyone meets once again in the cafeteria. The news that Tony had returned took everyone by surprise and was like waking up from a pleasant dream to a terrible reality.

Alberto listens silently to what happened in the morning. Lucia cries inconsolably as her mother tries to calm her down. Tony's ghost had returned and was much more aggressive since he was bringing Don Venancio and his gang of criminals with him. Alberto and Lucia had planned to announce that they would become parents but kept the secret to avoid any distractions that could compromise the operation they would launch to get out of Tony once and for all.

Vittorio tells Alberto. "Son, I told him I will study his plan and that I will answer him in two days only for you to tell us what to do. I do not know how to get out of this situation. Tony feels hurt and eager to recover everything he lost. The worst thing is that he has joined another mobster, so this is getting more complicated."

Alberto remained silent, and that makes the situation even more tense.

Vittorio stands in front of Alberto and, almost begging him, says. "Speak, son, say something. What are we going to do? We only have forty-eight hours; we have to prepare now."

Gregorio stops and interrupts abruptly. "Enough of so many problems. This is my fault. If I return to Italy, you will continue with your lives happily. It is me who has brought this problem and I must bear the consequences."

Gabriela takes her husband by the hand and says as a scolding. "Please sit down and stop saying stupidity. You don't know anybody in Italy."

Gregorio responds angrily. "I have cousins who still live in my hometown. They will help me; our family never abandons theirs own no matter how long they have been away."

Lucia looks at him with rage. "Father, you left Italy over fifty years ago. What the hell are you going to do there?"

Gregorio, besides feeling guilty, feels disempowered by his wife and daughter and angrily responds. "You better respect me, and that's my decision. There is nothing else to talk about."

Gregorio walks towards the exit and everyone looks at Alberto, who had not spoken a word all night. Only Alberto could change Gregorio's mind, so Lucia, without a second thought, says.

"Dad, listen to what Alberto has to say, and then you make your decision."

Alberto has no alternative but to take the reins again. He calls Gregorio and says.

"Gregorio, listen to your own words, which are very true."

Gregorio stops, turns around, and asks. "What do you mean?"

"You said that the family never abandons its own and we are a family. If you leave, you are abandoning us."

Gregorio, with tears in his eyes, responds. "No, son, I am not abandoning you. You will be with me always. I just want peace and happiness for you all."

Alberto gets up and gives him a hug. "Please sit down. Let's analyze a plan that I have in mind to get out of this nightmare all at once."

"Son, let's not go any further with this. We were lucky the previous two times, but this can change at any moment. Remember that now they are two gangsters, not one."

Alberto convinces Gregorio to sit down and listen to the plan. Alberto tells his father.

"Today you will contact Don Marcelo and ask him for information about that Don Venancio. Ask him to tell you about an incident that has earned Venancio fame or hate in the organization. You use that story in your next meeting with Tony to show him you are above Venancio. We will have Venancio and Tony eliminate each other, or at least to have Venancio eliminate Tony."

Gregorio, not convinced, answers. "That sounds very nice. But how will we get them to eliminate each other?"

Alberto shrugs his shoulders. "I don't know. That depends on the information we get about Don Venancio. What is certain is that I need you here with us."

That night, Vittorio called Don Marcelo.

"Hi Marcelo, it's me Vittorio."

"Hi Vittorio, I thought you had returned to Italy, by the way, I congratulate you on what you did to Tony. You are a professional. You portrait yourself as a saint and you are just like me."

Vittorio can't help laughing. "The truth is that I really enjoy fucking with Tony, but the idiotic one doesn't give up and keeps asking for more. I need your help once again."

Marcelo laughs out loud. "Listen Vittorio, if you want, you can work with me. I see you have talent."

"Thank you, but I must return to Italy. I just want you to give me information about some Don Venancio."

Marcelo surprised replies. "Be careful Vitto, don't play with fire. Don Venancio is a much smarter guy than Tony. He is a very cruel man who likes to eliminate his enemies personally. He kills and then finds out later. His strong business is in car theft. He gives out loans at a very high interest. I remember once that a client had fallen behind in payment and Don Venancio sent his bodyguards to bring the client to his office. The client swore to him he had sent him the money with his son, that there should be some explanation for the delay. Don Venancio did not want to wait and killed him with a shot to the head. A minute later, the client's son arrived with the money and apologized for the delay because he was involved in an accident. I thought he would feel remorse, but he told me he didn't have to wait for anything or anyone, that he was very clear with his clients when they asked and signed a loan."

Vittorio muted when he heard Venancio's story. His face was pale. Marcelo stares at the phone and asks.

"Are you there, Vittorio? I don't tell you this to scare you, but to let you know that you have to be very careful because you are entering another level and this guy is very dangerous."

Vittorio swallows, wipes the sweat from his forehead and, with a scared voice, responds. "Thank you, Marcelo, but I have no alternative. If I don't see you again, I want you to know that I am taking wonderful memories of you."

Marcelo, warmly, responds. "Vitto, I know you can do things that you yourself do not even think you can. Have faith in yourself and you see you will succeed as in the old days. Remember, you can count on me."

Alberto's business grew day by day, so the working hours became longer and to that was added the stress caused by Tony. Alberto knew that this was not good for Lucia, because so much stress could complicate her pregnancy. Alberto had taken two days to think of a plan which should put an end to this situation. Alberto tells his wife. "Love, let everyone know today we will meet in the cafeteria after we close the business. I also want to ask you not to take part. I want you to rest at home. This is not good for your pregnancy."

Lucia responds emphatically. "No, under no circumstances will I stop taking part in the meeting. This is a family problem and I want to be present and give my point of view."

Alberto understands he will not make her change her mind and decides not to touch the matter anymore.

Once gathered in the cafeteria, Alberto addresses everyone.

"We must be very careful. This time, we will be indirectly dealing with a very dangerous criminal. This can be productive if we don't make mistakes."

Alberto turns to his father and tells him.

"You will tell Tony that he must rent a warehouse because you cannot take the risk of storing the drug in the shipyard. You can only receive it at night and that same night, you must transport it to the warehouse. You will tell him that he must rent the warehouse three days before receiving the merchandise to make sure that the area is safe, and that Dino will stay in the warehouse all the time until all the drugs have been taken off the premises."

Then Alberto turns to Gregorio and tells him.

"You and Gabriela will pass by Benito's house again and leave a note in his car just as you did the first time. The letter will say that Lieutenant Clark killed your brother Caino by the orders of Tony and Dino. If you want to take part in the ultimate revenge, you just must put a FOR SALE sign on the back of your car with your phone number on the bottom. You will receive a phone call when the time comes."

Lucia asks Alberto. "What should I do?"

Alberto smiles and responds. "You will do the same as me, absolutely nothing."

Lucia, who had a notebook to write what each one should do, throws the notebook to Alberto, hitting him in the head and screams. "I'm not useless. I want to take part."

"Love you and I will be prepared in case of an emergency, and that's it." Alberto responds without reproaching her for throwing the notebook at him.

Gregorio and Gabriela try to calm down their daughter. "Lucy, Alberto is right, and he knows what he is doing. We must not fight among ourselves; we must be united."

"That's what I want, but they're taking me out of the group." Lucia responds angrily.

"Lucy, don't get stubborn like your mother." Says Gregorio.

Gabriela was eating soup and threw the spoon at her husband. "You are the stubborn one don't forget that all this is because of you."

Alberto hits with his fist on the table and everyone calms down. "What's happening? We can't fight each other and stop blaming Gregorio. He never meant to get us into this mess."

CHAPTER THIRTEEN

Tony Escapes to Turkey

A calm week had passed, like the relative calm before the storm. Lucia's pregnancy was being noticed, which was the incentive for everyone not to fight. One Monday morning, Tony shows up at the warehouse. On his face, there was great joy. The shipment should arrive on the weekend and with this he planned to make up for the lost money and to gain back the respect within the organization.

"Good morning, Don Gregorio. How are you?"

Gregorio is surprised to see how kind Tony has been to him, but he responds with equal cordiality. "Good morning, Don Tony, I'm fine, thank you very much."

Vittorio joins the meeting and orders Gregorio in a derogatory way to retreat.

"Gregorio, start organizing the boxes at the back of the warehouse. Tony and I have to talk."

Gregorio lowers his head and leaves, making Tony believe Vittorio is in control of the situation.

"I see you're happy. I hope you have good news." Vittorio tells him.

Tony raises his two hands upwards, as if thanking God.

"Yes, the merchandise will finally arrive on Friday night. I made some changes to maximize profits."

Vittorio opens his eyes as surprise. "That's good! Tell me, let's see what you have learned."

Tony fixes his tie as he used to do to show his arrogance and control over the situation.

"I decided that the shipment was not only marijuana like the previous two times. This time it will be 40% marijuana, 40% cocaine and 20% opium. This will diversify me into the market and is the reason delivery has taken so long. They will bring it on Friday night because you are closed on the weekend. It will be easier and safer to transport it."

Vittorio smiles and responds. "That you diversified is very good, but you can't leave the merchandise here. We've already had problems with the police in the past, and we don't know if we're under surveillance."

Tony moves his head in approval and asks. "You have more experience. What do you propose?"

Vittorio gives Tony a piece of paper and pencil and tells him.

"Write this down. I don't want you to say later you didn't know, or that I didn't tell you. You must rent a warehouse. That merchandise is not safe here and if you fail once again, that will be the last. Dino must stay in the warehouse until there is nothing left on the warehouse."

Vittorio pauses and asks. "Where is Dino?"

"Dino is in the car outside waiting."

Vittorio moves his head from side to side. "No, no, I want Dino here. He has to know of this."

Tony takes a deep breath, tries not to show his discontent and turns around and, without saying a word, leaves to look for Dino. Gregorio listened to the conversation behind some shelves and walks out with a smile from ear to ear.

"Vitto your true vocation is acting forget about mechanics."

Vittorio cannot control his nerves; his hands tremble and he is sweating profusely. "I just follow what Alberto told me, but I can't control my nerves. I am terrified, not for me, but for you all. If I make of mistake, one of you might get hurt."

Gregorio puts both hands-on Vittorio's shoulder and shakes him. "Good thing you can control yourself before Tony. I even think you are an old mobster myself."

Dino sees Tony approaching and asks. "What's going on Tony? Why that face?"

"This old man, I'm about to send him to hell. I'm not used to being treated like an idiot. After two transactions, we will be totally independent, and I will send him to fuck himself. I don't care if he comes from Italy or from another planet. Now come with me. The old man wants to talk to you."

Dino reluctantly gets out of the car and leaves with Tony to see Vittorio. As soon as Tony and Dino enter the warehouse, Vittorio tells Gregorio.

"I need you to go to the cafeteria and buy two breakfasts for our guests."

Gregorio looks at him with rage and responds. "I am not your employee."

Vittorio looks at him seriously and replies. "I was going to give you the money, but since you are so cocky, you are going to pay it now, you asshole."

Gregorio pretends to be angry and slams the door hard. Tony and Dino can't stand the laughter. Tony shakes his head in approval and says. "You have it tamed. You are a dangerous old fox."

Vittorio responds firmly, as if trying to teach Tony a lesson. "Never let a subordinate contradict you that erodes respect and always ends badly."

Vittorio then looks at Dino and says.

"Come over Dino. I want you to be aware of everything. I don't want mistakes of any kind."

Dino looks at Tony, thinking that Tony would intervene in his favor, but Tony also scolds to vent his frustration at not being able to send Vittorio to hell.

"Yes, come over and pay attention to this. This time you can't mess it up."

Dino moves his head in resignation, takes a deep breath. "I am all ears, sir."

Vittorio, dominantly, says. "We must transport the drugs the same night it arrives to the warehouse. You must be prepared to stay as many days as necessary in the warehouse. You won't leave the warehouse at all. Tony will bring you food and you must be armed."

Dino responds. "I am always armed and prepared, sir."

"What are you armed with, if I can ask?"

"I have my revolver always loaded and I bring extra ammunition in case of emergency." Dino replies, not willingly.

Vittorio slaps the counter, taking both by surprise. Tony, a little angry, intervenes.

"What is the problem now, Don Vittorio?"

"The problem is that you must prepare for the worst. That way, there will be no unforeseen event. If suddenly the supplier betrays us and wants to steal the merchandise, they will surely come armed to the teeth and will not go alone. If you respond to their revolvers with a machine gun, I assure you they will run away like rats."

Tony opens his arms with his fingers open. "Well, you're right, but I don't think the provider will betray us. He knows it would hurt his business and I would never let him go."

Vittorio extends his right arm and moves his hand with his fingers open. "No, no, no, Tony, if you have learned nothing yet, then I am out. I don't take unnecessary risks. No one will tarnish my reputation. Did you forget Caino betrayed you and then your famous lieutenant did the same to you?"

Tony takes a deep breath and looks at Dino, who dodges his gaze. "You are absolutely right, and I assure you it will be as you say. Tomorrow, when I go to Don Venancio, I will ask him for one of his machine guns and I am sure that he will not oppose because it is to take care of his own interest."

Vittorio opens his eyes in surprise. "I thought you already had the money."

"No, the less time I have Don Venancio's money, the better. His interest is too high, and he is very stubborn."

Vittorio laughs. "Well, that's your problem. I just want you to front me a thousand dollars. I want to invite you to celebrate our deal. I'm going to book a room in a hotel. I'll take five prostitutes and lots of champagne. I am tired of this boring life where I have to maintain a miserable profile. But I have already received the green light to return to Italy so that will be a farewell in style."

Tony smiles and replies. "That invitation belongs to me. Let me make it."

Vittorio responds bluntly. "That's a gift to you. You deserve it and I hope you don't fail me. The bosses have not allowed me to have money or have fun and I am like a child waiting for Santa Claus, but I will accept you on another occasion."

That night in the early morning, Gregorio and his wife put a note in Benito's vehicle and then monitored it to make sure Benito saw the note. Early in the morning, Benito leaves his house and sees the note in his vehicle. Benito sees the note and feels chills in his back, becomes paralyzed and looks around, trying to see something out of the ordinary, but not being able to find any clues. He takes the note. Benito takes the note with his right hand and starts tapping the left palm with the note several times as if thinking about whether to open it. Benito knew he had already avenged his brother's murder, so he was afraid to get involved in something that no longer interested him.

Gregorio and his wife looked at him from a distance and worried, because Benito was not opening the note. Benito enters his house without opening the note, so Gregorio must leave, only hoping Benito would open the note later.

Alberto, Vittorio, and Lucia were early in the business waiting for Gregorio and his wife, Gabriela. Lucia asked impatiently asks.

"How did it go? Did he read the note?"

Gabriela responds. "We don't know. He took the note and just looked around, trying to figure out who put it in. He looked nervous. After a while, he went inside his house with the note in his hand. That's all we know."

Everyone looks at Alberto, who has remained silent. "Say something, don't be silent. What is the plan B in case Benito does not respond?"

Alberto calmly responds. "Do not lose faith. He will open the note. I'm sure curiosity is killing him and if he doesn't respond, I'll think what to do next."

Vittorio angrily yells at him. "How is that you will think what to do then? This is not a game. Here we are all in danger. You can't improvise among thugs."

Alberto fixes his cap and responds. "Then think about it yourself, or any of you, because I have a lot to do. Today is a very busy day and I have to solve a lot of problems in the shipyard." Alberto leaves, leaving everyone amazed by the lack of attention that Alberto gave to the situation.

Gabriela angrily tells Lucia. "This is inconceivable how little importance he places to this matter."

"Well mother, Alberto knows what he is doing, and he has shown it very well."

"Of course, Lucy, you always defending your husband." Gabriela responds sarcastically.

"As if you didn't defend yours." Lucia replies.

A flushed Gregorio puts on his cap and leaves without saying a word. Both women stare at Vittorio, who doesn't know what to do. "What do you think of this, Don Vittorio?" Lucia question.

Vittorio puts on his cap and responds. "I don't know what to tell them. I don't have a husband."

Meanwhile, Benito had not read the note, but he had not separated from it either. He finally reads the note. Anyway, he didn't have to answer if he didn't want to be involved in something compromising. Benito opens and reads:

"Your brother's killer has been avenged. All that remains to do is to make pay the one who ordered to kill your brother. If you want to take part, you just must go to the same place where we were the last time next Thursday at 11:00 PM."

Benito broke the paper into little pieces and threw it in the trash. Then he kick the garbage while screaming. "You are also going to pay for it, I swear, by the memory of my brother."

Tony shows up on Thursday morning at Don Venancio's business and when he approaches Don Venancio's office, the door opens, and an employee comes out with a vehicle spare part in his hand. He tells Tony to wait a while because Don Venancio is busy with two customers. Tony arrogantly fixes his tie and looks at the all-grease-stained young mechanic and responds.

"I hope he doesn't take long; I don't have all day."

The young mechanic looks at Tony up and down and responds sharply. "Does he know you were coming?"

"No, but he knows who I am." Tony replies.

"I also know who you are. You can wait or you can leave."

Tony was surprised. He didn't expect such an answer. He had lost a lot of respect in the organization, but he never imagined that he had reached that low that a simple workshop mechanic would treat him like that. Tony thought of slapping him to teach him respect, but that would start the day on the left foot. Tony turned around and started looking at an advertisement on the wall to pretend that he didn't hear the young man. Tony sits down to wait, picks up a car magazine and starts looking at it when the office door opens abruptly. Don Venancio comes out accompanied by two thugs pushing the customer out. Don Venancio kicks the customer and yells at him.

"That alternator is not from my warehouse. I don't sell garbage. I sold you a car in perfect condition. If you want to return the car, is fine with me, but I will not return a penny to you."

The customer responds. "It's not fair. I gave you half of the money you asked me for the car and that was last week."

"That's your problem. You leave the car, and you don't owe me anything, or you take it and pay me the rest in three months."

The customer, almost imploring him, responds. "Don Venancio, you gave me a year to pay for the car."

"Yes, but since you want to be a smart ass, the rule has changed, so get out of here before you need an ambulance instead of a car."

The client left in a hurry and Don Venancio stares at Tony and says. "If I don't do it like this, others will want to do the same. Now tell me what you want. I thought you had changed your mind."

Tony lies to gain Don Venancio's trust. He smiles and responds.

"I have been very busy. After talking to you, I made two more transactions, by the way, very productive. If I come to see you, it is for two reasons. I gave you my word that we would do business together, and the second is that as the business has prospered and I am getting more merchandise. I will need your help with the security of the merchandise."

Venancio stares at him and replies. "Come into my office and we talk there."

Tony walks in and sits in front of Venancio's desk. Venancio takes some papers out of the drawer of his desk and practically throws them to Tony.

"Listen Tony, I will lend you the money, but there is no difference between you and any other client. I told you that before and I want to repeat it to you now once again so that there is no misunderstanding. As for security, I do not lend my men. If you think that the operation is not safe, then do not do it."

Tony responds quickly. "Don't get me wrong, of course the operation is safe. Only a little more security never hurts. If you can lend me a Thompson, I would appreciate it."

Venancio opens his eyes in surprise. "A Thompson! Are you going to war or what the hell is going on? I don't lend my guns or my men, but I'm going to make an exception with you. I'm going to rent you a Thompson for a week. Consider it an act of good faith. I will only charge you a hundred dollars and not charge you interest."

Tony responds, a little annoyed. "One hundred dollars! That's almost half of what it costs."

Venancio imposingly stands, puts his hands on the desk, and leans forward.

"Then buy yourself one, go to any pharmacy. I am sure they will sell you one without a doctor's prescription and maybe they even give you a discount for your pretty face."

Tony takes a deep breath and tries to control himself. He knows Venancio is an unpleasant and dangerous man, but he is the only one who has granted him a loan. "I want to tell you only one thing, Don Venancio."

Venancio stares at him and makes a grumpy face. "What's bothering you? We don't have to make any deals if you change your mind."

Tony gives a haughty response. "When you see that this operation produces more money than you can imagine, and decide to enter the business with me. You will have to take care of the safety and transport of the goods."

Venancio remains thoughtful and responds. "First, we reached the river and then we crossed it. Now I have no more time for you. Do you want the loan or not? Remember that it is a lot of money. I do not want surprises."

Tony takes the contract, and without reading it, signs it. "I know it's a high sum and your interests are abusive, but money won't be an obstacle in our relationship."

As was customary after closing the business, the family would meet in the business cafeteria for dinner and then go home. On

Thursday night after dinner, Alberto tells his father. "Tonight, we will go to meet Benito."

"How can you be sure that he will come to the appointment?" Gregorio asks.

"I don't know, but it's the only way to know."

"Let me go with you." Gregorio tells him.

"No, it will be better if my father goes. He already made the mistake of talking to Benito last time and that way he will realize that he is dealing with the same person and will be at ease. In addition, Papa is leaving soon for Italy so there is no chance that he will see him again."

Vittorio jumps quickly in his defense. "So, it wasn't a mistake for me to speak."

"Yes, it was. The plan was for you not to speak, and you didn't follow it."

"You weren't there, you do not know what was going on," Vittorio angrily replies.

Gabriela intervenes. "Alberto is right, the plans must be followed to the teeth."

Vittorio, with a shocked face, looks at her and then turns to Lucia and says.

"The lieutenant was about to kill your husband. I assure you that you would have screamed too. Or am I wrong?"

Lucia responds. "Yes, you are wrong. If Alberto said not to speak, you should not have spoken."

Vittorio moves his head from side to side and says. "Fuck! How bad it is not to have a wife to defend you."

Benito goes to the appointment but does not get out of his car or turn off the engine. In his right hand, he has his weapon ready for any unforeseen event and in his left hand, he holds a flashlight. Alberto and Vittorio were watching him. They arrived earlier to make sure no one else was around the place. It was a very dark and cold night. Few cars traveled at those hours of the night on that lonely road. All these elements made the scene more tense, since Alberto and Vittorio did not completely trust Benito, nor did Benito trust them. Vittorio approaches Benito's car and Benito tells him. "Stop! Hands up!"

Vittorio stops and Benito, without leaving the car, repeats. "I said hands up."

Vittorio doesn't know what to do. He didn't expect Benito to be more suspicious and aggressive than the first time. Vittorio raises his hands and keeps walking. Benito turns on his flashlight and lights Vittorio's face and then orders Vittorio. "Turn around. Let me see your back."

Vittorio responds. "You are armed, I am not. If I turn around, it is to leave, and we have nothing to talk about. If I had wanted to kill you, I would have done it the first time. The only thing I want is to give you the opportunity to close this chapter. If you do not want to do it, it's Ok with me. I have no problem, but this time it will not be like the first time."

Benito, confused, asks. "What do you mean by that?"

"The first time I told you that if you didn't want to take part, then I was going to take revenge alone, but that the lieutenant died that night. This time I will do nothing and not because I'm afraid. It will remain in your consciousness that the one that gave the order to kill your brother is still alive."

Those words gave strength to Benito, who opened the door and got out of the car defiantly. "I showed you I am not afraid to take part or to show my face. It is you who are afraid, and you cover yourself. I will not betray you. I would never do something like that, but you, with your mysteries, do not inspire confidence. Avenge my brother's death, but you might have some other reasons or your own interests."

Alberto had prepared his father for all the potential scenarios that might arise during the meeting with Benito, and that allowed Vittorio to speak with conviction and firmness.

"I understand you, and I owe you an explanation. I am a bandit, but a bandit with honor, just like your brother was. Because you will not tell me that your brother was a saint. If I cover my face, it is for my safety and also yours, even if you do not believe it. I had business with Tony for many years and met your brother when he was a young man. He was always very helpful and loyal. I had a great affection for him. He told me that Lieutenant Clark and Dino were robbing Tony. I talked to Tony, but he didn't believe me. Then Dino and Clark planted false evidence to incriminate your brother. That's why Tony gave the order to kill him, and Clark killed him in cold blood so that Tony wouldn't discover who the real rats were. I waited for the right moment to take revenge on Dino for the memory of my friend Caino. I take this risk because I do value genuine friendship and your brother was a loyal friend to me. I stopped doing business with Tony because he proved to have no vision of choosing his men and let them kill the only one who was faithful to him."

Benito screams. "Damn rat, I never trusted that dog. But what are we going to do with Tony? He also must pay?"

"When Dino falls, Tony is already finished. He has no one left. The organization itself will eliminate him, because the police will confiscate the drugs and Tony cannot pay back Don Venancio. This way, we will get rid of both of them."

Benito does not respond; he remains thoughtful for a while and Vittorio turns around and leaves. Benito asks him. "Why are you leaving?"

Vittorio returns. "This is simple. You take it or leave it."

"What do I have to do?"

Vittorio replies. "Listen well, there can be no failure, because your head also depends on it. On Saturday at 10:00 AM, come to this same place and you will find a note under a stone that will have a cross painted in red. The note will have an address, memorize the address, then go straight to the police and you will tell them you tried to rent a warehouse and that some armed men with their faces covered threatened to kill you if you appeared in the area again. You could see how they unloaded some sacks with what seemed to be drug smuggling, with a strong smell of marijuana. You will go with them and show them the place. Tell them that inside are the individuals because you just saw them enter. When the police arrest Dino, you leave so that no one sees you and you don't get into trouble. Questions?"

Benito answers. "Everything is clear now. Anything else?"

Vittorio responds. "Yes, if you ever hear my voice, for the sake of both of us, don't even dare to greet me."

Vittorio turned around and left, while Benito stared at him, until Vittorio got on Alberto's motorcycle and left.

Alberto arrived at the business with his father, everybody was waiting for them. Lucia and Gabriela ran towards them as if they hadn't seen him in decades.

"Thank God you came back; we were already going crazy. Did he show up for the appointment?"

Alberto responds, while trying to calm her down. "Yes, there is nothing to worry about. Everything came out as we planned."

Vittorio proudly says. "Alberto prepared myself for every possible scenario and I just followed the plan."

Gregorio sighs with great relief and asks Alberto. "How can you do all these things so naturally? I go crazy and I wouldn't know what to do."

Alberto smiles at him and responds. "It's very easy. I just put myself in Benito's place and this way I think about all the questions I would ask in his place. Then I think of the answers to all those questions based on our goal."

Gregorio can't contain his excitement and embraces him. "Thank you, son. I never imagined that you had such a talent. So, there was no mistake at all."

Alberto smiles and tells him. "That is why I make sure you stay here."

Gregorio pushes him. "More respect brat. I was already coming when you were planning on going."

Lucia responds. "Alberto is right and you are right, too."

Gregorio looks at her and, confused, asks her. "How is it we are both right?"

"Yes, there was no mistake because you did not go and when Alberto was planning to go, you were already coming from having fucking everything up."

Gabriela immediately reproaches her. "I don't slap you because you're pregnant, but you apologize to your father right now."

Vittorio says. "How lucky are these men that their women do not allow anyone to touch them!"

On Friday night, the drugs arrived at Alberto's shipyard. It was a dark night, but with excellent conditions for navigation. Gregorio plus the two men in charge of bringing the drugs unloaded the drugs from the boat. Tony and Vittorio were transporting the drugs into a truck rented by Tony and then to the warehouse where Dino was waiting for them. Dino joined them to unload the drugs but stayed in the warehouse as previously agreed. The operation took about four hours and two trips from the shipyard to the warehouse. Tony was excited. Everything was going perfectly, even the weather had been on his side. All the time, he told Vittorio about his future and that those plans did not include Don Venancio because he would not need his money.

When Tony, Dino, and Vittorio finish the last load, Vittorio tells Dino.

"Remember that you can only open the door to Tony, anyone else who approaches you open fire."

Everyone laughs out loud, and Dino shows him the Thompson machine gun he had prepared. Vittorio gives the two a firm handshake and tells them. "We are finally speaking the same language. I had my doubts, but I see the progress and I'm proud of what I see."

Tony was like a peacock. His dream came true. He believes that finally the alleged capo of the Italian mafia has recognized him. This blow would put him back among the most recognized, and that was just the beginning. Vittorio tells Dino. "I know that many times I have ignored you, but you have earned your position. Tomorrow, I invited Tony to celebrate as I usually do when I make a good deal. I promise you that when we finish here, we will celebrate my departure to Italy. Tomorrow, we will bring you lunch a little late because Alberto will be at the shipyard in the morning to deliver two boats."

Vittorio turns to Tony and asks. "Do you have my money?"

"Of course, Don Vittorio, here it is." Tony takes out the money and Vittorio replies.

"No, I just want you to buy two boxes of the best Champagne, then stop by a restaurant and buy a special meal and the best bottle of wine you can find for Dino. You know I don't have a car and I must keep a low profile until I leave. You are going to pick me up at the business at 1:30 PM. Alberto must have already left. We will come to bring the food and wine to Dino and then we will go to party until the next day."

"I have your thousand dollars and another five thousand that I got from the drug discount price I negotiated. So, if you want to keep the party for a week, we keep parting on me." Tony replies.

Vittorio laughs and replies. "No thanks, but I must leave in three days. I will continue the party on your behalf in Naples. You make sure you pay Don Venancio on time. That's a priority."

Tony adjusts his tie, as was his custom when something bothered him. "That old man will come to my knees trying to do business with me, but I'm going to give him back all his arrogance and make him swallow his insults."

Tony returns with Vittorio to the shipyard and says goodbye to Vittorio, who immediately calls Alberto and gives him the exact address of the warehouse where the drug is hidden. Alberto wastes no time and goes out on his motorcycle to put the note for Benito in the agreed place. They were very intense hours from that moment on. There was the possibility that Benito did not go the next day, so Alberto got there early and was watching remotely in case Benito does not show up. The time came and Benito did not appear. Alberto knew that getting involved in this operation could bring complications in the future, but there was no other alternative. After about 20 minutes past the agreed time and seeing that Benito did not show up, Alberto comes out of hiding and is about to get on his motorcycle when he sees Benito's car approaching.

Benito parks about fifty feet south of the agreed point and looks for the note. Alberto is about a hundred feet north of the agreed point, watching him with binoculars. Alberto sees Benito is disoriented and will not find the note, so he decides to go to the police himself. Alberto gets his bike on the road without being seen by Benito who was desperately looking for the note. Alberto is on his way to the police station, which was about fifteen miles south of where they were. Alberto slowly passes by Benito's side and can hear Benito cursing while looking around like a madman.

"Bastards, you want to drive me crazy? There is nothing here."

Alberto stops and tells Benito. "Hello, friend. Is your vehicle damaged? Need help?"

Benito looks at him and answers. "I don't your need help, go to hell."

Alberto replies. "Sorry, I just wanted to help you. Have a better day."

Alberto continues his way to the police station. Along the way, Alberto felt bad, because that night was very dark, so it would not be easy for Benito to find the spot two days later. Alberto had advanced about ten miles and was so deep into his thoughts he did not hear a vehicle coming at high speed, which when passing by, the wind almost pulled him off the road. Alberto recovers from the scare and gives full speed to his motorcycle, trying to find out if it was Benito's car. Alberto's bike could not compete with Benito's car, so he was left behind and he lost sight of it. Alberto continued because he did not know if Benito was going to the police or to his house.

Vittorio waited impatiently inside his room in the shipyard, staring at the clock on the wall constantly. "My God! Alberto has not confirmed that Benito showed up for the appointment and Tony is about to arrive."

Everything was calculated by time. The police should arrive before Vittorio and Tony arrived at the premises, but if Tony and he arrived at the premises before the police, then he would be involved with Tony. Tony knocks on the door of the business and Vittorio felt that the time had come for him to die, because having no news that meant that the plan had failed. Vittorio opens the door and sees Tony impeccably dressed and, with a smile from ear to ear.

"Are you ready for the party? I got two boxes of the best champagne we have and a bottle of wine for Dino. I also brought you from my restaurant Dino's favorite dish, as you asked me to."

Vittorio responds almost without strength. "Alberto left about twenty minutes ago. That asshole has made me suffer with his stupid boats and his parts orders. I can't wait to leave this place."

Tony responds. "Everything has its end in life and your days of poverty are over. Today is your last day on the job. Change that face. The party is about to begin."

Vittorio sighs and replies. "Son, at my age, after a day's work having to spend the night transporting drugs and then getting up early to work with this spoiled child, it takes away the desire for everything."

Tony had heard nothing Vittorio had said. He only cared that Vittorio had called him SON. That, for him, was the most important thing. Now he was regarded as a son to one of the mafia's bosses, he could not hide his excitement and happiness.

"Let's go Don Vittorio, change that face, come and see what I have in the trunk of my car." Tony walks to his car and opens the trunk, proudly displaying the two boxes of champagne.

"If you think it's not enough, I buy more. I have my contacts in the liquor store. The owner owes me several favors."

Vittorio is already expecting the worst. "No thanks, that's enough. Give me a few minutes to change and we will be on our way."

Tony returns to his car, turns on the music at full volume while singing and tapping on the steering wheel as if he was the drummer of a musical group. Vittorio takes the opportunity that Tony is in his vehicle to call Gregorio.

"Hi Gregorio. Have heard any news from Alberto? He should have called me, and he didn't."

Gregorio, surprised and worried, responds. "No, I know nothing about him, but if he doesn't communicate, please don't go. You can't be there when the police arrive. Please think of some excuse not to go."

Vittorio responds firmly. "I have to go. If I don't go, I will raise suspicions. I will think of something if I get arrested with Tony by the police."

"No Vittorio, don't go please." Gregorio pleads to him.

Vittorio hangs up the phone and calls Lucia. "Hello Lucia. Do you know anything about Alberto?"

Lucia worriedly responds. "No, Oh my God! What's going on?"

"Nothing daughter, I just wanted to talk to him." Vittorio responds, trying not to worry Lucia.

"If he hasn't called, is because there is a problem. Please don't go," Lucia responds worriedly.

Vittorio tries to calm down Lucia.

"I call you just to know if he was at home. You have nothing to worry about. See you later, daughter."

Vittorio gets out and goes to Tony's car. Tony was so cheerful and focused on his music that Vittorio must hit the roof of the car to get his attention. Tony gets out of the car as if he was the driver waiting for his boss. He does not miss an opportunity to ingratiate himself with Vittorio, who he thought was his ticket to the big leagues. "Forgive me, Don Vittorio. I was distracted with music." Tony opens the door, and he rushes out as if he was Vittorio's bodyguard.

The warehouse was about ten miles in a secluded industrial area. Tony was driving at low speed and kept asking Vittorio about his plans to return to Italy. "Rest assured, your percentage will remain the same. Even if you are not present, I will personally take it to Italy next year. If you wish, you can propose my service to the organization, and we will take this business to the planet Mars."

The music was so loud, and Tony was so focused on pleasing Vittorio that neither he nor Vittorio heard the sirens of four police patrols coming at full speed. Both give each other a tremendous scare when the patrols pass them by. Vittorio's frightened face helped him a lot not to raise suspicions.

"Fuck! What the fuck was that?" Vittorio exclaims.

Tony responds with a worried face. "I hope it's some fire or a fight at the damn Greek bar."

"Don't scare me, it better be. How far are we from the warehouse?" Exclaims Vittorio.

"We are about three or four miles."

Vittorio, with character, responds. "Then speed up, but without raising suspicions. I don't like this at all."

"Don't worry, Don Vittorio, don't spoil this special day."

Vittorio angrily replies. "I don't like this. I told you not to give the address of the warehouse to that man. He doesn't have to know where the merchandise is, especially if he already received his money."

Tony, trying to downplay the matter, responds. "Remember that this is the third time I have bought from that individual. I did it because I want them to transport the drugs to the warehouse themselves next time. That way, we don't have to have to do that work."

Tony and Vittorio exchange no more words. Everyone stays in place thinking about what might be happening. Tony asked God that these patrols had nothing to do with the warehouse, while Vittorio asked God for the opposite. Tony notices that the road is closed by the police. Tony stops the car, and the officer tells him he must turn around and that the road is closed. Tony turns around but stays by the side of the road. The officer approaches them and says, "I told you that the road is closed."

Tony worriedly replies. "I hope they open it soon; I have an appointment at the Greek bar."

"Well, you'll have to wait a while, because I don't know when this will be over." The officer responds and leaves.

Two more patrol cars entered the scene, and three ambulances also arrive at high speed. Vittorio and Tony are out of the car looking at the warehouses, trying to find out what happened, since the officers do not give any information. Many curious people gathered in the area since the police kept the road closed. About five minutes later, an ambulance escorted by two patrols left at full speed. Tony becomes increasingly impatient, walks from side to side and constantly asks the officers. Vittorio calls him aside and says quietly. "You have to control yourself. You're going to raise suspicions. We don't know what has happened there. It is a very large complex and maybe it is an unrelated incident, but your behavior can make things worse."

Tony takes a deep breath and responds. "You're right, but I can't help it. If anything has happened, it is not only a loss, but I also can't recover from it. It is a death sentence."

Vittorio puts his hand on Tony's shoulder and says. "I will not allow that; I've never turned my back on anyone who has done business with me."

Tony felt immense relief, almost kissing Vittorio's hands, who had to tell him to behave. An hour passed and because it was Saturday, many vehicles were heading towards the Greek bar and were waiting for the police to open the road. Suddenly, they realized a reporter had arrived and was preparing to give the scoop on the scene. Vittorio and Tony rush over to listen to the reporter.

"Good afternoon, I am Richard Blade from PBCS station reporting live from the scene where a shootout between the police and a heavily armed subject guarding a warehouse full of drugs has just occurred. I know that during the encounter, two law enforcement officers lost their lives, and a third is in critical condition. The drug trafficker who guarded the warehouse also lost his life. The names of those involved have not been released, and the investigation continues. The police keep the area sealed, so please avoid traveling on the industrial road until further notice."

Tony paled and was about to faint. Vittorio took him by the arm to prevent Tony from falling to the ground. "My God, it can't be possible. How could this happen? What do I do now?"

Vittorio tells him with character. "Compose yourself dammed, get in the car and let's get out of here. We have no time to waste."

Tony was walking to the car as if he was a sleepwalker dragging his feet. Tony gets to the car and stands next to the door, but he doesn't open it. He was totally paralyzed. Tony reacts with Vittorio's scream. "Open the dam door. What are you waiting for? The seconds count and can make the difference between your life and death."

Tony opens the door and they both get into the car. Tony puts both hands on the steering wheel. His eyes are lost and his face has the paleness of death. He turns and asks Vittorio. "What do I do now? Where are we going?"

Vittorio slaps him and yells at him. "Wake up, this is not the time to lower your guard. When the situation is critical is when you should be most awake and aggressive."

Tony tried to compose himself, but he couldn't help to reflect the terror that was consuming him. Vittorio orders him to go directly to the shipyard and hide his vehicle inside the business.

Tony looks at Vittorio and asks. "Can you explain to me what has happened?"

Vittorio replies. "Everything is very clear. Your provider knows you are easy to penetrate because the previous two times they had already done it. The last time was by Lieutenant Clark, so he knows there are police officer that can be recruited. When you give him the address of the warehouse, he recruited some police officer to steal the drug. Imagine you paid him fifty thousand dollars and the next day he steals the drug and sells it again. That is a phenomenal business, but they did not count that Dino was heavily armed and they paid dearly. Surely a shooting of such magnitude will be immediately reported by someone, and that is the result of not paying attention to me when I asked you not to give the address of the warehouse to that man."

Tony is sitting with his right hand holding his forehead. He moves his head from side to side without taking his hand off his forehead. "You're right. How could I not see it coming? The biggest problem is that Don Venancio must already know the news and must be looking for me. I am ruined. This was my chance to recover, but now I am a dead man. Don Venancio will not forgive a loss of such magnitude."

Vittorio, scratching his head to give more drama to the situation, responds. "Oh yes, you can be sure of that. If he finds you, he kills you, but I will not allow it. I will take you out of the country, but not Europe. It must be a place unknown to them."

Tony pulls his hand out of his forehead and looks at Vittorio as a plea. "But that's banishment."

Vittorio looks at him furiously and points his finger at him. "It's banishment or death. You can leave right now. I'm tired of your stupidities. I don't have children and if I was to adopt one, I assure you it would not be you."

Tony lowers his head and holds his forehead again with his right hand, totally defeated and totally at the mercy of Vittorio. "Forgive me, Don Vittorio. I will thank you for the rest of my life for what you are doing for me."

Vittorio replies. "The first thing you have to promise me is that you're going to listen to me and do everything I tell you."

"I promise you, Don Vittorio, I have already learned my lesson. I should have listened to you since the first time."

Vittorio is thoughtful for a moment, and Tony looks at him, waiting for an answer.

"Well, you must stay here and not move until I come back. Give me the keys to your car and take out the battery. I can't afford to have someone see you leaving here while I'm not here."

Tony didn't ask questions, gave him the car key and took out the battery. Vittorio takes a metal bar and hits the battery, making it useless. Tony opens his eyes and exclaims in amazement.

"What do you do that for? Now I don't have transportation."

Vittorio yells at him angrily. "Shut up. If I do this, is so you don't commit another stupidity while I'm gone. You will stay locked in my room; I am the only one who has a key. When I come back, I will knock on the door three times and then I will tell you it is me. If someone tries to open that door and it's not me, you shoot at the door. If you hear my voice without having heard the three knocks on the door, you also shoot. Is that clear?"

"Yes, Don Vittorio."

Tony enters Vittorio's room and Vittorio locks it and leaves on his motorcycle to Alberto's house.

They were all waiting anxiously for Vittorio. Lucia hugs him, and Alberto joins the embrace.

"Father, you do not know the scare that you have given us. Where is Tony?"

Vittorio responds. "Scare is the one you gave me by not communicating. Nobody knew about you and for a moment, I thought all this would have a terrible end for me."

Gregorio replies. "You are very stubborn. Lucia and I asked you not to go, and you lied to Lucia telling her you had communicated with Alberto. Why did you lie to us?"

Vittorio responds. "This had to end somehow. If I was arrested, I would have denied any knowledge about drugs. I would say that I was only accompanying Tony to a party and that he asked me to make a stop at that place."

Vittorio addresses Alberto. "Now tell me, what the hell happened to you that you didn't communicate?"

Alberto moves his head and responds. "I arrived early as we had agreed, and it occurred to me to add to the note a line that said; IF YOU DO NOT ARRIVE BEFORE 3:00 PM THE PLACE WILL BE EMPTY. Then I went back to my hiding place. Benito was late and could not find the note, so I decided to go to the police myself. I stopped and posed as a good Samaritan and asked Benito if he needed help with his car. He sent me to hell and kept cursing. I continued to the police, but Benito extended his search radius and found the note. Then Benito passed me in his car at such a speed that he almost threw me out of the road. I continued to the police because I did not know where Benito was heading to. When I arrived at the police, Benito was leaving the station with two police officers. Benito shouted at them, HURRY. Benito saw me and became enraged. One police officer asked me what I wanted. I replied I wanted to report a car that had almost killed me when it passed me at high speed. The officer asked me if I had information about the driver or vehicle's license plate and I replied that I only knew it was a red car. The officers didn't even answer me and went to get reinforcement. Benito came up to me and said furiously. STUPID ASSHOLD, I SHOULD HAVE RUN YOU OVER SO THAT YOU WOULDN'T BE SO GOSSIPY. I played frightened and apologized to him. Then I left at full speed. That's why I didn't have time to call anyone."

Gregorio asks Vittorio. "Where is Tony?"

"Tony is hiding in my room. He is demoralized."

Gregorio makes a gesture of victory by closing his fist and raising his arm upward.

"Yea! I'm glad, damn bastard. You don't know how I would love to see his face. But tell us what happened in the warehouse."

Vittorio surprised replies. "But you haven't heard the news?"

Everyone responds almost unanimously and curiously. "No"

"All I know is that a reporter broadcast from the scene and said there was a strong exchange of gunfire. Two police officers lost their lives, another is seriously injured, and Dino perished in the encounter."

Gregorio screams again. "Yea! Dam bastard."

Gabriela reproaches him. "Shut up. You shouldn't rejoice in anyone's death, even if they are bandits."

Vittorio asks Alberto. "What are we going to do with Tony?"

Alberto puts his hand on his father's shoulder and responds. "This has been a very tense day. No one has had even a bite of food. Let Tony take some of his own medicine and we have dinner here as a family."

"Very good idea." Gregorio replies.

"I cooked and brought the food, and no one wanted to touch it. I'm going to serve the table." Gabriela says.

Lucia hugs Vittorio and gives him a kiss. "Thank you. You can't imagine the relief I feel."

"No daughter, until Tony is not totally off stage we can't sing victory, but Alberto is right, let's have dinner first. Hey, you all, look what I brought you for dinner!"

Vittorio takes out the bottle of wine that Tony had bought for Dino and proudly lifts it up as if it was a trophy.

"My God! Where did you get that from? That wine is very expensive."

Vittorio laughs and responds. "It's courtesy of Tony. He bought it for Dino, but I think Dino has stopped drinking wine." Everyone was happy and sat down to dinner as if nothing had happened, remembered anecdotes from the old days, laughed, toasted, sang, and didn't realize how late it was. Vittorio looks at the clock on the wall and says.

"It's two in the morning. I think I must go back. Tell me, Alberto, what I do with Tony?"

Alberto stays thoughtful for a while and then responds. "Take him to the port. Try to contact a sailor from an Italian cargo ship and give him money to take him as a stowaway to another country. Make sure it's far away and not Italy. Tell him he cannot go to Italy because

Don Venancio would look for him there. I will give you money to negotiate with the sailor."

Vittorio responds. "No, he has money with him. He had planned a big party, so he will pay for his own ticket."

Alberto tells him. "Go before dawn, so that no one sees you. Many sailors return to the ships, most of them drunk and without money. If you get rid of Tony today, tomorrow we will all go to church to thank God. On Monday, we will not open the business. We will have a big party where we will celebrate our third wedding anniversary. We will invite all our employees and friends from the church."

Vittorio says right away. "I will buy the Champagne for the party."

"No, Vittorio, you shouldn't spend so much money. We're not in that condition." Lucia tells him.

Vittorio plays the offended. "No, Lucy, it is a satisfaction for me to contribute with my savings on an occasion like this."

Alberto approaches him and says in his ear. "You will tell them that, but I know you very well and I know how cheap you are. I am sure that it is not coming out of your pocket."

Vittorio returns to the shipyard and knocks three times on the door, and then tells Tony.

"It's me Vittorio I'm going to open the door."

Tony was behind the door ready to shoot and felt great relief when hearing Vittorio's voice. Vittorio enters the room and Tony asks him desperately.

"What happened? Why did it take so long?"

Vittorio sits and sighs as if he is exhausted and worried. "I was finding out, and Don Venancio has all his men looking for you. Ask to Don Marcelo to intercede for you and he flatly refused. Don Marcelo told me that Don Venancio is offering ten thousand dollars to the one who takes you alive before him and two thousand if they take you dead because he wants to kill you himself."

Tony swallows and, in a choppy voice, responds. "You promised to help me. You told me you wouldn't allow it."

Vittorio responds. "My word is unwavering. I will allow no one to touch you, but remember that you are indebted to me as long as you live."

Tony kneels before Vittorio and kisses his hand. "I am a grateful man."

Vittorio tells him. "Get up, put on my jacket and my cap so that no one recognizes you. We have no time to waste."

Tony gets up, gets dressed and, without asking where they were going, he gets on the back of Vittorio's motorcycle, and they leave the shipyard. Vittorio arrives at the port and tells Tony. "Hold on to me and walk as if you were drunk."

Tony puts his arm over Vittorio's shoulder and starts walking. Vittorio hears two sailors speaking Italian and immediately approaches them and asks.

"When and where do you sail?"

The sailor replies. "Why should I answer that question?"

Vittorio had taken the five thousand dollars from Tony, who had given it to him with no objection.

Vittorio takes out two bills of a hundred dollars and shows them to him.

"Here, I have two hundred reasons for your answer."

Right away, the sailor responds. "We set sail at 9:00 AM for Turkey."

"I need you to take my friend on the ship and dropped him off in Turkey." Vittorio tells them.

The sailors return his money and tell him. "That's complicated. We had to keep him hidden from the captain for a week. We won't take that risk."

Vittorio takes the two hundred dollars and adds it to the four thousand he had separated and tells them.

"How about two thousand reasons for each of you? That's much more reasons, than what you make in three months."

The sailors opened their eyes as if they had seen a ghost. They took the money from Vittorio's hand like lightning.

"These are enough reasons to take your friend to Turkey and bring the Sultan Suleiman from Turkey if you wish."

Vittorio has to try not to laugh. Vittorio puts a thousand dollars in Tony's pocket and tells him. "Use this money for you to settle down. Remember, you can't go to Italy, that would be your end."

Tony kisses Vittorio's hand again. "I promise Don Vittorio I will not return to Italy; I plan to make my life in Portugal."

The sailor asks Tony.

"Friend, you speak Italian?"

Tony replies. "Yes, I was born in Florence."

"Bravo, then sing with us and keep your head down."

They put Tony in the middle and walked away as if they were a trio of drunks.

Vittorio watched him get on the ship without raising suspicion, like a group of drunken sailors.

Vittorio returned to Alberto's house, as they had agreed to give him the news that Tony's ghost had ceased to exist. Everyone hugged each other and cried with joy to learn that they had finally freed themselves from Tony and his blackmail, they could finally live a normal life. They all stayed at Alberto's house and then went to church that morning. Alberto turns on the television to watch the morning news and they see they are interviewing Benito. Everyone runs to see the news; Benito is on camera being interviewed live.

"What can you tell us about what happened, since today, we learned it was you who killed the drug trafficker?"

"I went to the police station to report that masked armed men had assaulted me when I went to rent a place in the area. They told me that if I came back, they would kill me. I saw they were unloading what appeared to be drugs, and I went to tell the police. That is my duty as a citizen.

When I arrived at the station, I spoke to officers Roger and Wilson, who wanted to go alone, but I told them they needed reinforcements and so they called officers Martin and Glen. When they arrived at the scene, Roger and Wilson said they would go from the back and Martin and Glen would go knock on the door. I had followed them in my car because I wanted to show them where it was."

"Do you mean the police let you take part in the operation?"

"No, they asked me to leave, but I was curious to see what happened."

"And then what happened?"

"As I told you, Martin and Glen approached the door and were immediately killed. Roger and Wilson ran back to their vehicles. Roger took the radio of his patrol unit and immediately asked for reinforcement. He also informed they had two officers down. Roger did not finish the transmission when he was hit by a burst of gunfire."

"How do you know all this?"

"Because I was lying on the ground next to the patrol car and the door was opened. That is why I saw it and heard it all. Officer Wilson tried to answer the fire, but a revolver cannot compete against a machine gun. After firing six times, he had to reload his revolver and was then hit twice. Wilson fell to the ground, and the drug trafficker thought he had finished with everyone and came out of the warehouse. He had in his left hand the Thompson machine gun and in his right, his revolver. He approached the officers lying in front and kicked them to see if they were still alive, then followed to where Officer Roger was and did the same. I crawled on the ground slowly and took Officer Roger's gun without the dealer noticing me because he had his eyes fixed on Officer Wilson, who was groaning in pain. He stood in front of Wilson and asked him if he believes in God?"

"Yes, I am a believer, and I assure you that God exists." Wilson replied.

"Then he pointed his gun at officer Wilson's head and said. Well, go with God."

He was so focused on killing Wilson that he didn't hear my footsteps. Luckily, I shot first, and he fell on top of Wilson."

Wilson had closed his eyes, and when he heard the shot, he screamed. Then when I removed the bandit's body from him, he opened his eyes and realized that he was not dead."

What did Wilson say when he saw you?

He said. "Jesus!"

I replied. "It's not Jesus, it's me Benito."

The reporter turns to the camera and says. "The first reports showed the police had killed the drug trafficker, but later denied this version after the same officer Wilson corroborated Benito's version. The mayor of the city has given him the keys to the city and has labeled him as a hero."

"I only did what any citizen should do in such circumstances."

That morning after the religious service, Alberto and Lucia met with all the friends of the church who had supported them during the difficult times and invited them to the celebration of the third anniversary of their wedding which would be celebrated at Gregorio and Gabriela's house that same afternoon. It was a thrilling afternoon not only to celebrate their wedding anniversary, but to have freed themselves from Tony's blackmail. The party lasted until late at night, where Vittorio served an expensive champagne, courtesy of Don Tony. When the last guest leaves, Alberto says. "We must go to sleep because we have to get up early to open the shipyard."

Vittorio laughs and replies. "Nobody goes to sleep here; we all have to dismantle Tony's car and throw it into the sea."

Gregorio puts his hands on his head and screams. "My God, that man will never leave us alone."

The whole family went to the shipyard, where they worked without rest until they dismantled Tony's car and threw it into the sea.

Vittorio returned to Italy, and six months later, he returns with his wife for the birth of Lucia, who gave birth to a quadruplet who they named Albert, Victor, Greg and Lucy. The love of Alberto and Lucia overcame all the difficulties that fate threw at them, and the unity of the family helped them to overcome one of the most fearsome mobsters of their time.

END.